You don't know me at all.

You don't know the first thing about me. You don't know where I'm writing this from. You don't know what I look like. You have no power over me.

What do you think I look like? Skinny? Freckles? Wire-rimmed glasses over brown eyes? No, I don't think so. Better look again. Deeper. It's like a kaleidoscope, isn't it? One minute I'm short, the next minute tall, one minute I'm geeky, one minute studly, my shape constantly changes, and the only thing that stays constant is my brown eyes. Watching you.

you don't know me

a novel

DAVID KLASS

HarperTempest
An Imprint of HarperCollinsPublishers

Library of Congress Cataloging-in-Publication Data
Klass, David.
    You don't know me: a novel / by David Klass. — 1st
HarperTempest ed.
    p.   cm.
    Summary: Fourteen-year-old John creates alternative
realities in his mind as he tries to deal with his mother's
abusive boyfriend, his crush on a beautiful, but shallow
classmate and other problems at school.
    ISBN 0-06-447378-3 (pbk.)
    [1. Self perception—Fiction.   2. Interpersonal relations—
Fiction.   3. Child abuse—Fiction.   4. High schools—
Fiction.   5. Schools—Fiction.]   I. Title.
PZ7.K67813 Yo 2002   2002068518
[Fic]—dc21

Typography by Hilary Zarycky
❖
First HarperTempest edition, 2002

Visit us on the World Wide Web!
www.harperteen.com

For Giselle

1

who I am not

You don't know me.

Just for example, you think I'm upstairs in my room doing my homework. Wrong. I'm not in my room. I'm not doing my homework. And even if I were up in my room I wouldn't be doing my homework, so you'd still be wrong. And it's really not my room. It's your room because it's in your house. I just happen to live there right now. And it's really not my homework, because my math teacher, Mrs. Moonface, assigned it and she's going to check it, so it's her homework.

Her name's not Mrs. Moonface, by the way. It's really Mrs. Garlic Breath. No it's not. It's really Mrs. Gabriel, but I just call her Mrs. Garlic Breath, except for the times when I call her Mrs. Moonface.

Confused? Deal with it.

You don't know me at all. You don't know the first thing about me. You don't know where I'm writing this from. You don't know what I look like. You have no power over me.

What do you think I look like? Skinny? Freckles? Wire-rimmed glasses over brown eyes? No, I don't think so. Better look again. Deeper. It's like a kaleidoscope, isn't it? One minute I'm short, the next minute tall, one minute I'm geeky, one minute studly, my shape constantly changes, and the only thing that stays constant is my brown eyes. Watching you.

That's right, I'm watching you right now sitting on the couch next to the man who is not my father, pretending to read a book that is not a book, waiting for him to pet you like a dog or stroke you like a cat. Let's be real, the man who is not my father isn't a very nice man. Not just because he is not my father but because he hits me when you're not around, and he says if I tell you about it he'll really take care of me.

Those are his words. "I'll really take care of you, John. Don't rat on me or you'll regret it." Nice guy.

But I am telling you now. Can't you hear me? He's petting the top of your head like he would pet a dog, with his right hand, which just happens to be the hand he hits me with. When he hits me he doesn't curl his fingers up into a fist because that would leave a mark. He slaps me with the flat of his hand. WHAP. And now I'm watching him stroke your cheek with those same fingers. He holds me tight with his left hand when he hits me so that I can't run away. And now he's holding you tenderly with his left hand. And I'm telling you this as I watch through the window, but your eyes are closed and you couldn't care less, because he's stroking you the way he would stroke a cat and I bet you're purring.

You don't know me at all.

You think I'm a good student. Hah!

You think I have friends. Hah!

You think I'm happy with this life. Hah, hah!

Okay, now you're putting down the book that is not a book. It's a *Reader's Digest* condensation of literature, which is like drinking orange juice made from concentrate. It has no pulp. The key vitamins have been processed out. You're pressing your head against his shoulder. I can see your toes move inside your pink socks on the coffee table. What's with this toe movement? Is it passion or athlete's foot? There is some kind of serious itch there.

And now the man who is not my father puts down

his book, which is a real book, because he's not a stupid or shallow man, just cruel and self-centered. He kisses you long and full on the lips, and then on the side of your neck. And you glance upstairs, nervously, because you think I'm up in my room doing my homework. You don't know that I'm floating twenty feet above our backyard, watching this display of misplaced affection.

No, I am not levitating. I do not have secret wings that allow me to fly. I am not a vampire. I am not hanging by my heels from the roof or clinging to a drainpipe.

So where am I?

You don't know me at all.

I'll give you this one. I'm in the apple tree, which is not an apple tree. The man who is not my father calls it an apple tree, but it has never produced a single thing resembling an apple. Nor has it produced a pear, so it is not a pear tree. Nor has it produced a pair of apples. Nor has it produced a pineapple, so it is clearly not a pineapple tree. The only thing I have ever seen it produce is thin gray leaves, so I will call it a gray-leaf tree.

That's where I am. Sitting in the gray-leaf tree.

There's a full moon out tonight, so if I were a were-wolf or a vampire I would be hungry or thirsty for flesh or blood. But I'm full with the gluey spaghetti and golf ball meatballs from dinner. The only effect the moon has on me is to make me think of Mrs. Moonface and my five pages of algebra homework that is really her homework, except that for some reason I'm the one who got stuck with it.

Mrs. Moonface assigns us so much homework because she is miserable and lonely. I wrote a poem to her. It's not a very good poem, but I don't really care. The first stanza goes like this:

> *Mrs. Moonface, get a life,*
> *Get a nose ring, fly a kite,*
> *Find a boyfriend, learn to ski,*
> *Just stop taking it out on me.*

The man who is not my father is switching off the lamp. Now our house is dark except for the light in my room, which is really not a room, where I am not doing homework.

Except that I am actually up there doing home-work after all! Did you really think that I was up in the branches of an apple tree? Not necessary. You don't have to see things to know that they are happening. Anyway, I don't like climbing trees. It's a cold fall night. The wind is howling around our house like a live animal.

I finish the last algebra problem. Put down my pencil.

Downstairs I can hear the springs of the couch creaking. The man who is not my father is repeating your name, with passion in his voice. But it's not really your name, even though it belongs to you. It's really the name of his pretty first wife, Mona, who died in a car accident five years before he met you and decided to move into your house, and take on the duties of disciplining your son.

And now he is repeating your name and thinking of Mona.

And you are listening to him and thinking of my father.

And I am not in this house at all. I am in the middle of a hurricane. Thunder is cymbal-crashing above and beneath me. Lightning makes my hair stand up. Winds are spinning me like a top. Do you really think I will come down to breakfast tomorrow and call the man who is not my father sir? Do you think I will go to school tomorrow and hand in my homework to Mrs. Moonface? I won't even be in this hemisphere tomorrow. This storm could set me down anywhere.

You don't know where I'll end up.

The good news is that you may have created my past and screwed up my present but you have no control over my future.

You don't know me at all.

2

anti-school

This is not school, this is anti-school. If school and this place ever came together there would be an explosion that would destroy the entire universe.

How do I know that it's anti-school?

School is a fun place and this place is torture.

School is for learning and this place is for becoming stupid.

This place doesn't even have a library, and who ever heard of a school without a library?

I'm sitting in the middle of third period of anti-school, in anti-math class, listening to Mrs. Moonface go over the problem sets. Here is what she is saying:

"The coefficient of *a* multiplied by the divisor of *c* yields the identity of the variable."

Here is what she is really saying:

"I do not wish to be Mrs. Moonface and I hate

algebra as much as you do. I really wish to be a Hollywood movie star and have my own trailer with mirrored walls and a sandwich tray delivered every hour by a handsome man named Jacques."

Mrs. Moonface, you will never be a Hollywood star. You could assign sixteen thousand pages of algebra homework and you would not become a Hollywood star. You are Mrs. Moonface, named after the lunar surface, by me, for obvious reasons that have to do with the color of your skin and the roundness of your chin. And I am John, named after a toilet, by my father for reasons that are not so obvious. He could have called me kitchen. He could have called me living room. He named me John.

Next to me is Billy Beezer, whose name is really Bill Beanman but who I have rechristened Beezer on account of his nose, which is three times longer than seems natural, and which I have nicknamed Beanman's Beezer. He could be an aardvark, which is a kind of anteater that lives in the front of the dictionary. He could be a sloth, which is a tailless mammal that eats, sleeps, and travels upside down. But he is neither aardvark nor sloth; he is Billy Beezer, my friend who is not a friend.

He is not a friend because we are both in love with the same girl. Her name is Glory Hallelujah and she is the ugliest girl in our entire anti-school. She is so ugly her mirror tries not to look back at her in the morning. Her hair is so greasy that lice ice-skate on it. She is also the stupidest girl in our anti-school. She is so stupid that she might actually like me.

Okay, I'll give you the truth here. Because it's important. Her name is not Glory Hallelujah but Gloria. She is not ugly at all.

In fact, she is the most beautiful girl in our anti-school. She is also smart as a whip, whatever that means. I just pretend that she is ugly because I am thinking of asking her out on a date, and when she says no I want to be able to tell myself that I didn't really want to go out with her anyway, because she is so ugly.

Billy Beezer is also thinking of asking her out on a date, but he is too self-conscious about his long beezer to ever actually do it.

"John," Mrs. Moonface says, "can you tell us the lowest prime number that is also a factor of forty-eight?"

No, Mrs. Moonface, I can tell you a lot of true

things, but I cannot tell you that. I can, for example, tell you exactly the way Glory Hallelujah's ankles are crossed at this very second, right on top of left, with her white socks stretched up taut almost to her knees. I can tell you that Billy Beezer is smart not to ask her on a date, because she would laugh at him, whereas she would never laugh at me, even if she said no, which she will never say, because I will never get the courage to ask her.

"John, are you thinking? Are the wheels turning?"

I can also tell you, Mrs. Moonface, about this African tribe I was reading about in *National Geographic* called the Lashasa Palulu who, when they are in their homes, walk on their hands so that they will not leave footprints in their houses. No, that is a lie. There is no such tribe. But it's not a bad idea. The man who is not my father WHOPPED me yesterday for leaving mud tracks across the kitchen that is not a kitchen.

It is not a kitchen because it cannot produce a good meal. Nothing resembling edible food has ever been prepared there. Surely, if it were a kitchen, something good to eat would eventually come out of it. That is the definition of a kitchen. It must be a bedroom or a bathroom masquerading as a kitchen. This is the problem with my house. None of the rooms are what they seem to be. My bedroom, for example, is not a bedroom, because I cannot sleep in it. I suspect it is a closet, because it's so small.

"John, we can't wait forever . . . ?"

Anyway, Mrs. Moonface, I was crossing the kitchen that is not a kitchen when the man who is not my father grabbed me so hard his fingers dug into my shoulder and he shouted, "Look what the hell you're doing!"

And I looked down. There were four or five muddy footprints on the linoleum floor, and by coincidence and bad luck they happened to be about the same size as my feet. Now, if I were a Lashasa Palulu, this would never have happened, because I would have been walking on my hands. But since I am who I am—a person you don't know, and will never know—they were there, and I got WHOPPED. A WHAP is a slap to the arms or body, and WHAPS hurt badly enough, but a WHOP is a hard smack to the back of the head that makes your eyes see red and yellow, and makes your ears ring.

"So," the man who is not my father said, "I guess

you'll think twice about tracking mud through the house again."

Now, if I were a Lashasa Palulu, I would probably have kicked him in the nose, because one advantage of walking on your hands is that it leaves your feet free for combat, but since I was not born into that tribe that is not a tribe, all I could do was start to cry, because the WHOP hurt so much.

"Go ahead and cry," the man who is not my father said. "You make me sick."

So I cried, because making him sick seemed to be the only way I could harm him, and, frankly, because I couldn't stop myself. It hurts to cry like that when you don't want to do it, in front of someone you hate.

Every tear burns.

"Look at you," the man who is not my father said, "just look at you. You'll never be a man. Quit blubbering. I *said quit it*." And he WHOPPED me again, even harder.

"John?" Mrs. Moonface asks. "Are you with us? Are you in the Milky Way galaxy? We're running out of time."

Mrs. Moonface, obviously I cannot answer your question, because my ears are still ringing from the

13

two WHOPS, so why don't you select another member of the studio audience? The man with the hat, or the woman with the false teeth, perhaps . . .

"John, do you even hear me? Are you not well?"

Billy Beezer gives me a hard elbow in the ribs. "Doofus, just say you don't know. You're making an idiot of yourself."

But, thankfully, at that moment I am rescued by Glory Hallelujah, who raises her hand and at the same time calls out the correct answer to Mrs. Moonface's question without any hesitation, thereby saving me from eternal doofusness.

"That's correct," Mrs. Moonface says, with an approving look to Glory Hallelujah.

Glory Hallelujah gives no obvious sign that she knows she has saved my life. She doesn't look at me. She doesn't say anything to me. But what she does do next is brush her blond hair off her neck with her left hand, which can only be a secret signal to me.

I scratch my right ear, which is the secret answering signal of gratitude.

That is when I decide that I will ask her out on a date.

3

band practice

I do not play the tuba. The tuba plays me.

My tuba is actually not a tuba, because it has never produced a musical sound. It is actually a giant frog pretending to be a tuba. Every so often it forgets that it is pretending to be a tuba, and it gives a loud croak that causes Mr. Steenwilly to jerk his head around so fast he nearly gets whiplash. He looks at me with his baton quivering in the air and his mustache quivering on his upper lip, and I know what he's thinking. "You are killing this piece of music," he is thinking. "You are murdering this song. You should be arrested by the music police. They should hang you from a music stand."

Mr. Steenwilly, I cannot argue with you—I am murdering this piece of music. That is a fact neither of us can dispute. But surely you must understand that I cannot get a musical sound out of what is really a giant frog pretending to be a tuba. I move my fingers and blow my lungs out. Occasionally it croaks.

No one is to blame here.

Furthermore, Mr. Steenwilly, I do not wish to be here any more than you wish me to be here. Band practice is not my idea of a good time. Music is not in my blood. I do not sing in the shower. I do not whistle in the dark. I cannot sing on key. I cannot even sing off key. Mr. Steenwilly, I cannot sing, I cannot whistle, and I cannot possibly play a tuba that is really not a tuba.

You just gave me that look again, because the tuba that is not a tuba just played a note that is not a note. In fact, I believe it was a bullfrog croak that means "I'm hungry. Where are the insects in this pond?" I admit that there are no hungry bullfrog croaks in this march by John Philip Sousa, but the salient point here, whatever that means, is that I am not to blame.

Let me repeat that, because it is an important message for the whole world to hear: I AM NOT TO BLAME.

The frog seems to have gone to sleep in my arms, and no sound at all is coming out of the tuba that is not a tuba. I will continue to puff my cheeks and move my fingers, but this is a good chance for me to clear the air with you about why I am here, Mr. Steenwilly.

The only reason why I am here is because in our anti-school there is a rule that everyone must participate in one extracurricular activity. Now, I couldn't play football, or any other sport, because I'm too strong and fast and well coordinated and I would embarrass all the other athletes, and impress too many girls, and then everyone would hate me for being such a success.

I couldn't join the Student Council because it's really not a student council in that it has never provided counsel to any students or accomplished anything positive for anybody. It's really a group of students nobody likes, who try to get elected to completely meaningless but impressive-sounding positions so that they can put "leadership skills" down on their college applications. Billy Beezer is on the Student Council. He and I ran against each other in our homeroom and everyone felt sorry for him on account of his long beezer, so he won and I lost. Of course, I am glad that I lost because I did not really want to be on the stupid Student Council anyway.

I couldn't be in the Glee Club because I have no glee. There is nothing resembling glee that I know of in any way connected to myself. Even if I had glee, I would not join the Glee Club, because glee is like money—if you have it you should hide it, you should stash it in the bank, you should not wave it around.

But I don't have any glee. I don't have any money either, by the way.

I couldn't be in the French or Spanish Club because I am having a hard enough time mastering English.

I could go on, but I think you get the picture, Mr. Steenwilly. The reason I am in your band room, holding on to a giant frog that is pretending to be a tuba, is because the process of elimination has brought me here. There is nothing I am better at than not being able to play this tuba that is not a tuba.

Pathetic? Perhaps. But truthful.

You, on the other hand, have many other places to go. I know all about you, Mr. Steenwilly. I read an article about you in the paper. You have an advanced degree from a famous conservatory. You were a brilliant pianist. You won prizes. So what are you doing in our anti-school, teaching students like me and like

Violet Hayes, who sits in front of me trying to play the saxophone? I have nicknamed her Violent Hayes because she appears to be trying to strangle her saxophone before it kills her. This is perhaps justifiable, because I believe her saxophone is not a saxophone at all. I say this because it has never produced a sound like a saxophone. I believe it is a monitor lizard pretending to be a saxophone.

So there you stand, poor Mr. Steenwilly, tapping your foot and waving your baton while sweat runs through your thinning hair, and in your mind you are hearing lovely John Philip Sousa. But in your ears you are hearing car crashes and hungry frog croaks and monitor lizard shrieks. And my point is this. I believe you are on a crusade here, and you are doomed to failure.

You will spread no light at our anti-school. You will be engulfed by darkness. Get out while you can.

We are done with John Philip Sousa. We have moved on to a piece written by Arthur Flemingham Steenwilly. Your parents must have really hated you to give you such a name.

The piece you have written for us is called "The Gambol of the Caribou." Now, Mr. Steenwilly, I don't mean to be critical. What I know about music could be squeezed into a peanut shell, and there would still be room for the peanut. But I looked up "gambol" in the dictionary, and it means to "skip or jump about playfully." It also means to "caper or frolic." Caribou are large, ponderous, woolly reindeer.

They do not gambol. They do not caper. They do not frolic. And they certainly do not skip. It would be an interesting sight to see a herd of caribou skipping down the tundra, but, Mr. Steenwilly, it would never happen. You could write a piece called "The Caribou Standing Still and Freezing Their Butts Off." Or "The March of the Caribou." Or even "The Stampede of the Caribou." But "The Gambol of the Caribou" is not such a great image to build a piece of music around.

I hope I haven't offended you, Mr. Steenwilly. But I think you may have a problem in this area. Because several months ago you gave us another one of your original compositions to play, and it was called "The War Cry of the Ostrich."

Now, the ostrich is a fascinating bird, but it's not exactly known for its battle prowess. When an ostrich is threatened by an enemy it feels such terror that it can't bear even to watch whatever bad thing is happening, so it sticks its head in a hole in the ground and awaits its fate, blind, deaf, and trembling.

Now, I grant you, Mr. Steenwilly, it's possible that the ostrich is yelling down there in that hole, but I think it far more likely that it's bellowing its bird lungs out in terror than uttering a battle cry. If you had called your piece "The Panic Attack of the Ostrich" I wouldn't have had a problem. Or "The Last Hysterical Screech of the Ostrich."

Now you are waving your arms for the final crescendo of "The Gambol of the Caribou." The caribou must be gamboling pretty intensely in your mind. But in the real world of the band room, it sounds like a disaster movie. In front of me, Violent Hayes and her saxophone that is really a monitor lizard are trying to get at each other's throats. Behind me, Andy Pearce is banging on the drums that are not drums. They sound like a car crash. I can hear fenders collide and iron rip.

Meanwhile, the frog in my arms has awakened. He lets loose with a sound that has never appeared in the Western musical canon. In fact, it sounds like something has just been shot out of a cannon. Is that why you spin around so fast your mustache trails your chin, Mr. Steenwilly? Are you afraid you will be blasted by cannon shot? The good news is that you have nothing to fear from military projectiles.

The bad news is that the final few bars of your musical composition do not sound like any animal capering and frolicking. They sound like an avalanche in a war zone.

And even though some of the most horrible sounds the human ear is capable of registering are coming from my direction, I am not making these sounds. They are being made by the frog pretending to be my tuba. I used to wonder what he was doing hiding in a band room, but I have developed a theory that may explain everything.

The giant frog may believe that he is in a band, and that I am a tuba. Sometimes I can feel him blowing back through the mouthpiece, and even moving my fingers on the keys. Which is why I say that I do not play the tuba—my tuba plays me.

Band practice is over. Please go into your band office and have a nice cup of tea, Mr. Steenwilly. Please do not stand there glaring at me. Please do not walk over to me as you are now doing. I will focus on putting my tuba that is not a tuba into its case, thereby deflecting your anger. Why don't you glare at Violent Hayes, who has just barely survived another encounter with her saxophone.

You have stopped in front of me. "John, I would like to speak to you in my office."

"Yes, I would like to speak to you too, Mr. Steenwilly, but I have chemistry next period, and it's on the other side of the school, so . . ."

"I let everyone go five minutes early. There's plenty of time. Let's talk. Now. In my office."

4

get me out of here

I have called chapter 4 "Get Me Out of Here" because that is precisely what I am thinking as Mr. Steenwilly ushers me into his band office and closes the door behind us.

He is smiling, which I take to be a bad sign. "Please, sit, John," he says.

So I sit.

"You have unusual technique when it comes to your tuba," he says with a grin.

I nod.

"Highly unusual."

I nod. "Thank you."

"This is going to sound crazy, but sometimes I swear it almost looks like you're talking to it, and treating it as if it's alive."

I manage to smile back at him. I even manufacture a little laugh. Mr. Steenwilly, you are far too smart to be teaching at our anti-school, and you are far too smart for me to handle one-on-one in your office like this. This would be a very good time for a fire drill—or a flash flood.

"You don't practice much at home, do you?"

"I guess not as much as I should."

"John, it's none of my business, but is everything all right at home?"

"Sure." "Sure" is a very good word for situations like this. It's like a little shovel you can use to dig yourself out of a hole.

"Because you were wearing a T-shirt the other day and I could have sworn I saw some red marks on your arm and shoulder. They looked like someone had been grabbing you. And I wondered . . . I mean, are you positive that everything is okay?"

"Sure."

"Because if something is going on, and you need help, I want you to feel that I'm someone you can come to."

"Sure. Thank you, sir. Right now I should get to chemistry lab . . ." I stand up.

"John, to hell with chemistry lab."

I sit down. We look at each other.

"You have sad eyes, John," Mr. Steenwilly finally says. "You remind me a lot of myself at your age, which is probably not a good thing for you."

Nor for you, Mr. Steenwilly.

"Let me tell you about myself at your age. My father wanted me to be a doctor. I wouldn't have made a very good doctor, John. I hated the sight of blood. Frankly, I was a little lost. I didn't have many close friends. I spent a lot of time inside my own head."

This is fascinating, Mr. Steenwilly, but perhaps you should keep it to yourself. I do not wish to hear about your childhood. You think I am some kind of kindred spirit, but I am not. You don't know me at all.

"Those were good years, John. Frankly, I muddled through them, but I didn't enjoy them. Childhood is golden. I don't mean to say that you are a child, but I do think that, as the ancient Greek playwright said, every day in the light is precious. They're especially precious when you're young. It's a special time."

Mr. Steenwilly, among the Lashasa Palulu, child-hood, as you call it, is seen as one long obstacle course to be survived. There are wars with other tribes during which children's heads are prized trophies. There are the cold winters. There are the blistering

26

summers. There are the leopards that live in the forest and feed on young men and women who cannot run fast enough. When a Lashasa Palulu reaches adulthood, they never think or talk about their early years. It is like their childhood was a void, a big zero. What is important is that they survived.

"John, are you listening to me?"

"Yes, sir."

"You looked like you were far away. You don't have to call me sir. We're not in the army, here, are we?"

"No, Mr. Steenwilly. I'm listening."

"John, I don't believe it's a healthy thing for a young person to spend so much time inside his own head. It's a trap. One I know all too well. Now, one way out of that trap is to find a magic portal to the outside. For me, John, music was that magic portal. Does this make any sense?"

Mr. Steenwilly, to be honest with you, all I want is to get out of here. I am nodding and listening and saying "sure" but the only magic portal I am interested in is the one out of your band office.

"When I found music, John, all kinds of things opened up for me. The world became a more beautiful place, a warmer place. I became more confident. I made friends more easily. Even girlfriends." Did you just wink at me, Mr. Steenwilly, or is there something in your eye? "But the reason all these good things were happening was because I was enjoying my life. Do you see what I'm getting at?"

Mr. Steenwilly, I see you sitting there beneath two large posters—one of Beethoven and one of Brahms— and I must tell you, you still don't look very happy to me. You still have sad eyes. And neither of them looks very happy either. "Sure, Mr. Steenwilly. I really need to get going now."

"I didn't know you were so fond of chemistry."

"I just don't want to be late. I'll get detention."

"You still have plenty of time. Before you go, John—do you have anything to say to me?"

I am searching for a good answer. Nothing in my pockets. Nothing up my sleeve. Seconds tick away. "I'm glad you found music, Mr. Steenwilly. I'm not sure I'll ever be really good at it, the way you are."

"Let me make a suggestion to you. The next time you play a piece of music, don't think of it as a jumble of notes. Try to think of it as a story. Put it into words, in your mind, if that helps. Or put it into pictures, like a movie. Or even think of it as series of colors or emotions. Will you try that?"

"Sure." I am standing. I have almost dug myself out of the hole.

"Good. Because we're going to start playing a new piece soon, and you're going to have a solo."

Mr. Steenwilly, are you nuts?

"I know you can handle it."

So you are nuts. Next question: Why must I pay for your insanity?

"Now, go enjoy the rest of your day. And if there are ever any problems at home, you know who you can talk to."

"Sure."

losing by a snout

We are hanging out at the Bay View Mall, and Billy Beezer, my friend who is not a friend, is talking about food. "I'm so hungry I could eat a whole horse," he says, "from snout to tail." This is another reason why Glory Hallelujah would never go out with him. Billy Beezer talks about food all the time. When he is eating a piece of chicken, he is already eyeing another piece of chicken on his plate. While he eats lunch, he talks about what he will eat for dinner. I have seen him eat a large pepperoni pizza, and then a plate of spaghetti with meatballs, and also a loaf of garlic bread, and get up from the table looking hungry. He is a bottomless pit.

Despite the fact that Billy Beezer eats all the time, he remains as thin as a pencil. This defies several of the basic laws of physics. If every action has a reaction, then every mouthful should produce weight.

My theory is that all the food he eats gets sucked into the vacuum tube of his long beezer and from thence hurled into an alternate universe.

Billy Beezer is in a hungry state as he, Andy Pearce, and I ride down the escalator at the Bay View Mall. His stomach is growling like a wolf cub in a snow cave.

It is called the Bay View Mall even though it does not look out at any bay. In fact, it does not look out at anything. Inside the Bay View Mall are two department stores, a dozen or so specialty shops, a pet store, a movie theater, and a food court.

The escalator drops us off in front of the food court, and Billy Beezer's tongue starts licking his upper lip, and his eyes start to glow. We pass Hot Dog Man. We pass The Pizza Barn. We pass Wong Chong Panda Express, where a cook is stacking egg rolls in a steamer tray on the counter.

Billy Beezer is flat broke. I can see his fingers checking the corners of his pockets, but there is nothing there. Not even a penny. Only lint.

"You think I'm kidding, but if you left me alone with a dead horse, a knife, and a hot plate, I swear I could finish it off," Billy Beezer says, his eyes on the

31

egg rolls. "Horse steaks probably taste like beef. Just give me some A.1. sauce and hide the saddle scars. I could eat the hooves like pig's feet—pickle 'em and suck out the juicy bits. I could eat horse eyes—fry 'em in oil like pumpkin seeds and crunch them between my teeth. I could even eat the snout."

"Horses don't have snouts," Andy Pearce says. Andy is the drummer in our band, with the unique musical talent of making the end of every musical composition sound like a car crash. I have not given him a nickname because there is nothing about Andy that is at all remarkable. He always wears the same clothes—blue jeans and a faded T-shirt. He takes everything he hears literally, and everything he says has exactly one very obvious meaning. He is not stupid, but he has only one gear, which can get tiresome.

The only reason I am hanging out with him and Billy Beezer is—as you have probably guessed—because I take pity on the two of them.

"If horses don't have snouts, what do you think they smell with?" Billy Beezer wants to know.

"Noses. Horses have noses," Andy Pearce informs him. "Pigs have snouts."

Billy thinks about this while his eyes fix on a giant pretzel in Salt Heaven. "What do you know about horse noses, Nerf brain?"

Andy Pearce shrugs. "When they're calling a horse race they say 'He won by a nose.' They never say 'He won by a snout.' "

"When have you ever been to a horse race?"

"I have heard them on the radio and watched them on TV, and they never say 'Won by a snout.' They say 'Won by a nose' because horses have noses."

It is impossible to win an argument against someone like Andy Pearce. He will destroy you with obvious statements.

Billy Beezer can't stand the temptations of the food court any longer. With a last look at the egg rolls in Wong Chong Panda Express, he leads us to the down escalator, which deposits us on the ground floor, opposite Pete's Pets.

There are three kittens in the window of Pete's Pets, and there are three girls about our age looking in at the kittens. The three of us get off the down escalator and look at the girls.

We do not know these girls and they do not know us. They must be from another town and another school system. Therefore, they do not realize that they should run for the hills at the sight of us. They do realize that we are looking at them from a distance of about fifty feet. They whisper to each other and pretend to focus on the kittens.

"Eight o'clock—three babes," Billy Beezer announces in an excited whisper. Apparently, the sight of the girls has taken his mind off food. "They're checking us out big time."

"No, they are looking at kittens," Andy Pearce corrects him.

"And why do you suppose they are pretending to pay so much attention to some scrawny kittens, doofus face?" Billy Beezer demands.

"Maybe they're thinking about buying a kitten," Andy speculates logically. "They could be trying to decide which one to buy."

"They're shopping all right," Billy Beezer tells him, "but I guarantee you it's not for pets."

"Then why are they looking in the window of a pet shop?"

Billy Beezer is getting exasperated. "Because they don't want us to know that they're checking us out. Get it?"

"Do I get what?"

"Do you get tired of being such an idiot?"

"No, it doesn't make me tired."

Among the Lashasa Palulu, when a group of young men are going on a raiding party and an argument breaks out among them, one member of the raiding party takes it upon himself to restore order. This job usually falls to the son of the chief, or to some other young man of notable intelligence and dignity.

Clearly, the time has come for me to intervene between Andy and Billy Beezer and create some order from the chaos. "They were studying those kittens before we got here, so it's possible they're thinking of buying one," I say. "But they are also checking us out because they are trying to decide if we are worthy of them."

"Yeah, well, I'm trying to decide if they're worthy of me," Billy Beezer says. "I don't see them winning any beauty contests. In fact, they better not stand too close to that pet store or someone may try to buy them."

At that moment, the three girls disappear inside the store. "Come on," Billy Beezer says, "they want us to chase them."

We follow him over to Pete's Pets and walk inside. It is not a big store. There are fish along one wall in tanks. Birds along the back wall in cages. Reptiles and turtles along the third wall in terrariums. And in a center section are little plastic apartments with glass doors and toy furniture, and puppies and kittens inside of them.

The three girls are standing in front of the reptile section, looking in at a grass snake. The tallest of them is saying, "Oooh, look how slimy he is. I think he just munched on a fly. Is that a fly head hanging out of his mouth?"

"I think maybe it's a cockroach," her friend who has braces says.

"Oooh, gross, disgusting," says the third one, stealing a quick look at the three of us. Hopefully, she is talking about the snake.

We are pretending to look at a tank full of neon tetras. "They like us!" Billy Beezer whispers. "They're into us, major league! We should go over and break the ice."

"I don't see any ice," Andy Pearce says.

"We should go over there and talk to them, mud mind, before we lose our moment," Billy Beezer says.

He would like to go over and say something to them, but he is embarrassed because of his enormous beezer. No one has handed me the envelope with the correct opening line, so I also hang back. I tell myself I must remain loyal to Glory Hallelujah. I cannot wander around malls trying to strike up conversations with girls I don't even know.

"I'll go talk to them," Andy Pearce says. "It's no big deal." And he heads right over.

Billy Beezer flashes me a look that says "God only knows what will happen now!" but he follows Andy. I trail along a short distance behind, trying to strike a difficult balance. If Andy Pearce is somehow success-ful, I want to be part of the group, but if he makes an ass out of himself, which seems more likely, I do not wish to be associated with him.

Andy Pearce has no fear. He walks right up. "Hello," he says to the three girls. "Are you thinking of buying that snake?"

The tall girl looks at him. "No way. It's gross. Why on earth do you think we would buy that thing?"

"Because you are looking at it," he tells her.

The tall girl looks confounded for a second.

"And this is a pet store," Andy Pearce continues.

"The animals here are all for sale."

Billy Beezer and I exchange a look. Perhaps Andy knows what he is doing. Or perhaps the girls will misinterpret his statements as sarcasm or cool charm. Or perhaps they will head for the hills.

The girl with the braces jumps to the aid of her friend. "So what are you doing here?" she asks.

"Talking to you," Andy Pearce replies with Vulcan-like logic.

The third girl gives Andy a flirtatious smile. "So, are you a snake?"

"No, I am a human being," Andy tells her.

The three girls giggle and exchange worried looks at the same time. They cannot figure out what to make of Andy. "How come you three human beings came over to talk to us three human beings?" the third girl asks him.

Andy Pearce hesitates for a second. "My friend said I should come over here and break the ice," he finally says, "but I don't see any ice."

Now the three girls look like they are starting to catch a bad scent. But they're still not sure.

"He's joking. He's a real kidder," Billy Beezer says, trying to inject new life into the conversation. But his stomach chooses this moment to growl. It is a loud and disgusting sound. It is no longer the sound of a wolf cub in a snow cave. It is the sound of a ravenous polar bear in a penguin sanctuary. Billy Beezer puts his hand on his stomach as if to cap an explosion, and at the same time he looks to one side, as if to suggest that the sound came from one of the reptiles.

The three girls do not know what to make of this intestinal eruption, and they still do not know what to make of Andy Pearce.

"Were you being wise about that ice stuff?" the tall girl asks Andy.

"No, I am not wise," Andy tells her. There is an expectant lull. They are looking at Andy. Waiting for him to say something. I can tell that he doesn't have a clue what to say next. "But I do know that the best place to find ice is an ice machine," he finally says. "There are no ice machines in this store." Now that he has found a topic he is comfortable with, Andy plunges on recklessly. "The best place to find ice machines is in hotels. People need ice to bring to their rooms. They fetch it in ice buckets."

Now the three girls have realized that Andy is not being cute or clever or sarcastic. He's just being himself and they had better head for the hills. You can see it in their faces. "We have to go now," the tall girl says.

"Yeah," her friend with braces says, "we have a ride waiting. Bye."

"If you find the ice, don't fall through it," the third one says to Andy, and they hurry out of Pete's Pets, and burst into laughter as soon as they are outside.

Now the three of us are by ourselves, staring at the grass snake. I believe the insect that is still hanging out of its mouth is a beetle. We can hear the girls laughing as they run away. Billy Beezer points a finger at Andy. "You are from Pluto. What did you think you were doing?"

"Telling them about ice machines," Andy Pearce replies.

"Yes, you did a very good job of that," Billy says. "You have the brains of an ice machine."

"Leave him alone," I say. "At least he talked to them. That's more than either of us would have done."

Billy Beezer doesn't like hearing the truth. "I would have said something."

"No you wouldn't," I tell him. "Neither would I. We are both cowards, when it comes to that. So leave him alone."

"I am not a coward," Billy Beezer responds. Apparently I have pricked his pride. "You'll see how much not a coward I am tomorrow morning. Now I'm getting out of here."

The girls are gone. The coast is clear. We exit Pete's Pets. Billy Beezer and I step onto the escalator. Andy Pearce rides up behind us.

"What happens tomorrow?" I ask.

Billy gives me a long look. There is a warning in his eyes. My friend who is not a friend is telling me that he is going to do something that I will not like. "Tickets to the Holiday Dance go on sale."

"So?"

"I'm going to ask Gloria," Billy Beezer announces.

"You will never have the guts to ask her to the dance."

"True. But I don't plan to ask her to the dance right away, doofus. I'm going to ask her to the basketball game Friday night against Fremont Valley High. And she'll go because she loves basketball."

"What makes you think that?" I ask casually, but now I'm worried. Because Billy Beezer has a plan. A sly plan. An incremental plan.

"Her brother was a star high school player, who

41

now plays on a college team," he says. "And I heard Gloria tell Valerie Voss that she wants to go to the game this Friday. So it's a slam dunk."

I don't say anything for several seconds to my friend who is not a friend. We just look at each other. I am thinking, "Gloria cannot go to the Holiday Dance with you because she will go with me."

"I'll ask her tomorrow in homeroom," he says. "You don't see her till third-period math class. By then she and I will already be an item. Deal with it."

An item? It sounds like something stacked in a grocery, like a can of peas. "I liked Gloria first," I say. "I talked about her to you first."

"Tough eggs," Billy Beezer says as we step off the escalator. "All's fair in love and war. And speaking of eggs, I'm going to get myself an egg roll from Wong Chong."

"You can't," Andy Pearce says, joining us. "You don't have any money."

"There's more than one way to get an egg roll," Billy tells him. We are approaching the food court. Billy lowers his voice. "Now, here's what you do," he tells Andy. "Go up and ask the guy how much a Chop Suey Combo is."

"I don't want a Chop Suey Combo," Andy Pearce says.

"But you might someday," Billy points out.

"That is true."

"And then ask him how much an Egg Foo Young Platter is. And keep asking questions. Do it now."

Among the Lashasa Palulu, the mere knowledge that an illegal act is taking place does not make a person guilty. One must participate in some way to be guilty. Therefore, innocent but curious, I watch the action unfold from a safe distance.

Andy Pearce walks up to the cook in Wong Chong Panda Express and asks how much a Chop Suey Combo is. And while this is happening, Billy Beezer sidles up to the other side of the counter, where the egg rolls sit in a steamer tray.

"Chop Suey Combo, four dollars," the cook says.

"And how much is an Egg Foo Young Platter?" Andy asks.

"Four dollars. You want Egg Foo Young Platter?"

"No," Andy says. "But how much is Orange Chicken?"

"No Orange Chicken."

"Do you call it Orange Chicken because of the

color or the flavor?" Andy asks.

"No Orange Chicken. You want General Tso's Chicken?"

While this illuminating discussion is taking place, Billy Beezer seizes his moment, reaches a long arm around the counter glass, and grabs an egg roll out of the steamer tray.

Unfortunately for Billy Beezer, the heat on the steamer tray is cranked up pretty high. Which means that the egg roll is piping hot. Billy burns his hand and gasps, "Aaaah!"

It's not a loud gasp, but it's loud enough for the cook at Wong Chong to pivot around and shout, *"Stop! Thief! You steal my egg roll!"*

Caught in the act, Billy Beezer has only two sensible ways of proceeding. He can drop the hot egg roll on the counter and bolt. If he does this, I doubt the cook at Wong Chong will bother to chase him. Or he can pull out his wallet and pretend he meant to buy the egg roll all along. Of course, he has no money, but it is not a crime to forget that you have no money.

Billy Beezer opts for a third course of action. Holding the hot egg roll in his right hand like a relay racer's baton, he turns and flees.

The Wong Chong cook vaults the counter with unexpected gymnastic ability and gives chase, yelling, *"Stop! Thief!"*

Billy Beezer is not particularly fast, but the Wong Chong cook does not possess world-class speed either. They both appear to be running in slow motion as they race around the food court. They vault tables. They upset chairs. They nearly knock over an old woman, who screams and pulls a fire alarm.

Billy Beezer is heading for a service elevator. The doors to the service elevator begin to close. If he makes it, he will get away. If he doesn't, he will be cornered. He is pumping his arms. He throws himself forward. I think he is going to make it. But just as he reaches the elevator, the doors shut tight. He pounds his fist against them.

The cook from Wong Chong grabs him by the arm. Billy struggles and kicks him in the leg, but the cook spends all day hacking up ducks and dicing pork, and he has a grip of iron.

I am fifteen feet away. Despite the fact that Billy Beezer said "Tough eggs" to me a few minutes ago, I might try to help him, if I could think of a way. But I cannot. And at that second, a big, fat, bald mall cop waddles up. "What's going on here?"

"*He stole my egg roll,*" the Wong Chong cook shouts.

"*No way,*" Billy shouts back. "*I did not.*"

The mall cop looks down at Billy's hand, which is still clutching the egg roll. "Did you pay for it?"

"Not exactly," Billy says.

"Then how did you get it?"

Billy is stuck. "I don't know," he says. "I just got it. I mean, now it's in my hand. But I don't want it." He tries to hand the egg roll to the mall cop. "Here, take it."

The mall cop glances down at the egg roll. Judging by his girth and the look on his face, he wouldn't mind a quick snack. But of course he is in his official capacity. "Do you want to press charges?" he asks the Wong Chong cook.

"Yes. He kick me. I press charges."

And at that moment the old woman walks up. "This boy ran me over," she says. "I saw the whole thing. He's nothing but a juvenile hoodlum. I want to press charges, too."

The mall cop takes out some handcuffs. Billy

Beezer begins to cry. The mall cop puts Billy up against the closed service elevator door and begins to cuff him.

Poor Billy Beezer. Even though he is turned away from me, I can tell that he is suddenly very scared. His knees are knocking against the elevator doors. If he had been one step faster, he would have made it through those doors, and gotten away with his crime.

But he didn't make it. He lost. By a snout.

dinner theater

I am sitting at our table that is not a table, trying to eat a turkey dinner that is not a dinner, and ignore the mayhem. "The mayhem" is my name for our Tuesday dinner entertainment, which the man who is not my father has selected for our enjoyment and edification, whatever that means. He is seated to my right, sawing away at a turkey leg that is not a turkey leg, his eyes never straying from the TV screen.

The food on his plate and, sadly, my own plate can in no way be classified as a turkey dinner because it fulfills none of the basic requirements of a true turkey dinner: it does not taste like turkey; it does not look or smell like turkey; it does not even have the consistency of turkey. Nor does it taste like chicken. Nor does it taste like any member of the fowl family. Nor does it taste like beef, pork, or lamb. It also does not taste like a vegetarian dish cleverly flavored and decorated to resemble turkey. I do not believe that what I am eating has ever experienced life as we understand it in any form, animal or vegetable, bacterial, or even viral. I suspect that what sits on our table that is not a table may in fact be a rare whitish-gray mineral masquerading as turkey.

Our table is not a real dining room table because real tables are flat, whereas ours lists to one side like the deck of a slowly sinking ship. Every week or two the man who is not my father will get his big tool kit out and prop up one leg, or saw off another, and then use a marble to show that the table is finally level. "There," he says, "solved that problem. Hah!" But since it is not a real table, but rather a ship that is slowly sinking into our dining room floor, it will soon be tilted again.

There is a roar from the TV. The mayhem is intensifying.

The TV has become a royal figure in our house since the man who is not my father moved in six months ago. We used to have a small TV that sat on a crate in a corner of the living room. When the man who is not my father arrived, his one contribution in terms of furnishings was a brand-new wide-screen color TV with its own oak stand—a king presiding on a dark wooden throne.

I am sitting next to the man who is not my father, trying to gulp down a few bites of our turkey dinner that is not a turkey dinner, and trying to ignore the fact that Tiger Jones has just broken the nose of Vinny the Fox.

"Yup, it's broken," the announcer says with apparent satisfaction. "I could hear the bones snap. His cornermen really have their work cut out for them. Lucky he's got Doc Whittaker in there—one of the best cut men in the East. And he's gonna need him, because blood is now gushing from the nose and eyes of Vinny the Fox!"

Now, since you don't know me at all, even though you are starting to get a picture of the ridiculous world in which I live, I will reveal a surprising secret about myself. Despite my many drawbacks and human frailties, I am not particularly squeamish. I do not grow faint at the sight of blood, unless it is my own. I am not troubled by images of stark violence, unless that violence is heading in my direction. But that being said, I hold this truth to be self-evident: no one, while eating dinner, should be forced to watch a

50

fellow human being get his nose broken.

The bell sounds for the end of round five. Poor Vinny the Fox staggers back to his corner, where he is stitched and glued back together by Doc Whittaker. The camera moves in close on Vinny's nose and eyes.

I try not to watch, but there are a limited number of places that I can focus my gaze on in our dining room that is not a dining room. It is not a dining room because no good meals are ever eaten in it. If you will excuse a gross word, I believe it may be a vomitorium masquerading as a dining room. I say this because I frequently feel nauseous during meals. And I am feeling nauseous now, as I try not to look at the screen, and consider my other options.

First, I can look down at the whitish mineral on my plate that is pretending to be turkey. This is not a good way of curing nausea because I believe the whitish mineral may be a powerful emetic, whatever that means.

Second, I can look at the man who is not my father. He is almost done with his turkey leg, although he has actually managed to ingest very little of it. Some of it has fallen from his fork onto the tabletop, where it has accumulated in dribs and drabs around his plate, like the first spotty snowfall of winter. Larger pieces, fearing to be eaten, are clinging desperately to his mustache, or have wedged themselves between his irregular teeth like mountain climbers seeking shelter in ice caves.

The man who is not my father feels my look.

"John, sit up straight," he barks. But what he is really saying is "Who are you to stare at me? Have you forgotten who rules this particular roost? I can remind you with my right hand as soon as your mother isn't around."

"Okay, sorry," I say, and make just enough of a minor modification in the alignment of my upper vertebrae to satisfy him, but what I am really saying is "I will not snap out a 'Yes sir' to you, which I know is the phrase you would like. You may be bigger and older and meaner than I am, you may be my tormentor and the man who has done such a poor job of replacing the man who named me after a toilet, but I do not accord you the rank of commanding officer.

"I will, however, stop staring at you, as the process by which you eat turkey that is not turkey is making me sick."

So I look away from the man who is not my father,

at our dog, Sprocket. In one of the great ironies of my life, our dog Sprocket is indeed a dog. He smells like a dog, acts like a dog, and has the loyalty of a dog. The first time the man who is not my father hit me, Sprocket growled at him. The man who is not my father kicked Sprocket in the head. Although I have not seen it because most of the day I am away at school, I suspect the man who is not my father beats Sprocket even more regularly and more severely than he beats me. I say this in part because Sprocket gives the man who is not my father more and more space.

Sprocket is now curled up in the doorway, eyes closed, listening to us try to chew our dinner. Of course, if we were eating a real turkey dinner, Sprocket would be under our table, wagging his tail and salivating, but since we are eating a mineral pretending to be turkey, Sprocket could not be less interested.

Tonight I cannot look at Sprocket for long. His dog's snout reminds me of my friend Billy Beezer, who I last saw less than an hour ago, being escorted out of the food court by two mall policemen and a real policeman with a badge and a gun. At this moment, while I am eating my turkey that is not turkey, I believe that Billy Beezer is being interrogated by the foremost experts in criminology in our region.

This is another possible reason why I am nauseous.

Billy Beezer may crack.

He may name names.

He may name my name.

Billy Beezer doesn't know who I am any more than you do, but he does know my name and address.

Now, it is true that among the Lashasa Palulu, unless you actively participate in committing a crime, you cannot be held in any way responsible. But unfortunately, I am not under the judicial authority of that tribe that is not a tribe.

I do not pretend to be an expert in the conspiracy-to-commit-egg-roll-theft laws of this particular neck of the woods. It is, for example, possible that merely having been present at the Bay View Mall, in the company of Billy Beezer, can get me into trouble. Perhaps at this moment Andy Pearce is going down for his role as Wong Chong chef distracter, and I will be the next domino in the chain to fall. It has even occurred to me that Billy Beezer may try to shift or at least spread the blame for his crime.

I am waiting for a knock on our door. I am listening for the sound of sirens in the night. If the colored lights of a police car were suddenly to make a Christmas pattern on our window curtains, it would not surprise me.

So, for all the above reasons, I do not want to look at Sprocket and his dog snout, which bears such a marked resemblance in shape and size to Billy's beezer that it is tempting to believe that Billy's ancestors—by some great and heinous indiscretion—must have assimilated some canine genetic material.

So there is only one other place I can rest my gaze as I finish my turkey dinner that is not turkey, and try not to watch Vinny the Fox get eviscerated, whatever that means.

I am watching you.

You don't know me at all, but I know you well. I am familiar with every line and crosshatch in your so very tired face. I know the way you slice your entire meal up in little pieces before you eat it, as if you are nearing the very end of your strength, so you need to do all the hard work first.

I can see the blurriness in your eyes. You do not have my problem of figuring out where to rest your gaze during this meal that is not a meal. You are barely conscious of the mayhem. The man who is not my father's table manners do not appall you, because you do not see him clearly. You see him through a filter of tiredness and nostalgia that makes him look to you just like the man you married when you were twenty years old and full of hope.

I have seen you in that wedding picture, standing next to the man who named me after a toilet.

You have more than just hope in that photograph, which is now hidden away. You have more, even, than youthful beauty. You have glee. Your eyes glow.

I did not know you then, but I know you now, and I can see clearly what lies at the bottom of the long slope that you have tumbled down. You have raised the white flag. You have surrendered to the enemy without terms.

The only question that remains is whether your surrender was at all justified and deserving of sympathy, or whether it was a cowardly and despicable act.

This is a difficult question. In deciding it, I must not be cold or unfeeling, or selfish to your sacrifices and suffering.

You think I don't know what it is like to have a husband you love disappear on you? Hah! I know it very well. I learned it from listening to you sob late at night. I understand it because I myself have a hole in my heart for the man who named me after a toilet and never stuck around to explain why.

You think I don't know what it is like to work a double shift on an assembly line at a factory? Hah! I know it very well, because I know you so well. I can see it in the way your whole body sags, right down to your fingers loosely holding the silverware. I can hear it in the way you breathe when you first come home after work, in so many small sighs, as if even your lungs are exhausted. I can even understand it in your need to be stroked and petted by the man who is not my father. It is pitiful, but comprehensible.

Yes, I understand it. I can even be sympathetic to a point. But here is the essential truth, which I hold to be self-evident: an unconditional surrender cannot and should not be arranged without consulting all the other officers in your army.

I am not just a part of this house. I am not just a brick in the wall or a beam in the roof or the welcome mat that is so frayed the word "welcome" looks like "Don't come."

57

Neither am I the doorbell or the brass lion's-head knocker, although both are capable of making sounds. I am also not the dog curled up in the dining room doorway, although he is alive. I am not even the TV set, even though it has wheels and can chase us around the house, and is the only altar the man who is not my father worships at.

I am more than any of these. I am a person, a person you clearly do not know, and will never know. I have a full voice here. I have my rights here. It may be your house and I may live in a room that you own, but I have rights and must be heard!

The mayhem suddenly swells to a crescendo. The man who is not my father leans forward with his elbows on the table and gives a loud belch.

Vinny the Fox is being counted out. The ref waves his arm and signals that the fight is over. Vinny evinces no detectable signs of life at all. Doc Whittaker climbs into the ring and bends over Vinny, but there is nothing he can do. He is a cut man, and I believe Vinny the Fox needs an undertaker.

Our dinner that is not a dinner is over.

I get up from the table and clear my plate. I also clear the plate of the man who is not my father. And

I clear your plate. I carry plates and silverware and glasses into our kitchen that is not a kitchen, and scrub and sponge and stack and dry.

You are wrapping up uneaten turkey for a future meal that will not be a meal. We are alone in the kitchen. The man who is not my father does not believe in a division of labor among all members of the dining group. He is still seated at our table that is not a table, waiting for Vinny to be scraped off the mat so the next fight can start.

Did you not hear a single word I said, O my tired and worn mother? I'm right here, next to you. I see you so clearly—how can you not see me? Are you that deaf or that beaten down?

Or is it rather, as I have suspected all along, that you do not know me at all?

7

Torture Island

It's strange how an entire day, or even a week, can become focused on one precise instant.

I am sitting in anti-school, in anti-math class, with a piece of paper in my hand. No, it is not my algebra homework. It is not a quiz that I have finished and am waiting to hand in to Mrs. Moonface. The piece of paper in my hand has nothing at all to do with mathematics. Nor does it have to do with any school subject. Nor is it really a piece of paper at all.

It is really my fate, masquerading as paper.

My right hand is damp with sweat. I did not know that my hand was capable of sweating this much. I have folded the paper that is really my fate up into a neat, small square and now I am holding it in my damp palm and waiting.

I am sitting next to Glory Hallelujah and I am waiting for a break in the action. Mrs. Moonface is at the front of the room, going on about integers. I am not hearing a single thing that she is saying. She could stop lecturing about integers and start doing a cancan kick or singing a rap song and I would not notice.

She could call on me and ask me any question on earth, and I would not be able to answer. If she asked me what color grass is, or what my name is, or how many ears I have on my head, I would not be able to answer.

But luckily, she does not call on me. She is in lecture mode. She has a piece of chalk in her right hand. She is waving it around like a dagger as she spews algebra gibberish at a hundred miles a minute.

I hear nothing. The sound waves part before they get to me and re-form when they have passed me by. Algebra does not have the power to penetrate my feverish isolation.

You see, I am preparing to ask Glory Hallelujah out on a date.

I am on an island, even though I am sitting at my desk surrounded by my classmates—except for Billy Beezer, who is noticeably missing from school today.

I am on Torture Island.

There are no trees on Torture Island—no huts, no hills, no beaches. There is only doubt.

Gloria will laugh at me. That thought is my lonely and tormenting company here on Torture Island. The exact timing and nature of her laughter are open to endless speculation.

She may not take me seriously. Her response may be an honest "Oh, John, do you exist? Are you here on earth with me? I wasn't aware we were sharing the same universe."

Or she may be sarcastic. "John, I would love to go on a date with you, but I'm afraid I have to change my cat's litter box that night."

She may read my note, cover her pretty mouth with her delicate hand, turn redder and redder with the strain, and suddenly explode with uncontrollable laughter like Mount St. Helens erupting right in the middle of anti-math class.

Or, worst of all, she may disguise her laughing refusal beneath layers of pity: "John, it's so sweet and brave of you to ask. I'm sure there are dozens of girls who would be thrilled to go out with you on Friday night. I have no doubt that you will grow into a tall, handsome, rich, and successful man, and at the tenth reunion of our anti-school I will eat my heart out for having turned you down."

But what she will really be saying is: "That may all happen in the future. But in the here and now you are a hopeless dweeb, named after a toilet, and I am Glory Hallelujah—how dare you even think that I might allow us to be seen together in a social situation?"

So, as you can see, Torture Island is not exactly a beach resort. I am not having much fun here. I am ready to seize my moment and leave Torture Island forever.

I have a plan to leave. It is a bold plan. It could work.

There is only one problem. Mrs. Moonface must cooperate with my grand design and create some space for me. She must turn completely away from us and begin writing formulas furiously on the blackboard. That will in turn compel all the students in anti-math class except me to begin copying furiously in their notebooks. Hence a double void will be created—a hole in space and time, if you will—that I can use to seize my moment and escape from Torture Island.

I will at that precise second lean over and tap Glory Hallelujah lightly on the shoulder. Or perhaps I will tenderly nudge her elbow. Or it may be that I will blow a cool stream of air, like a zephyrous autumn wind, whatever that means, across her cheek. She will turn her lovely features in my direction. Our eyes will meet. My right hand will rise slightly and come forward in the universal gesture of friendship and note-passing. She will deftly take the note from me, our fingers brushing slightly, magically, in the process.

She will unfold my note in her lap, like a secret treasure map, and read it with a single glance from her flashing blue eyes. And then she will look up at me, and I will have my answer in an instant, and whatever that response is—good or bad, pleased or angry, willing or unwilling—I will be off Torture Island.

I guess you are probably wondering what is written on the piece of paper that I am holding in my right hand.

I confess that I did not sleep last night. I lay awake in my bedroom that is not a bedroom, staring at the ceiling, and pondered strategy and tactics as a great general does before a battle. There are not many ways of asking a girl out that I did not consider and discard.

I had not hit on a method I liked when I arrived at school this morning. In fact, I had drawn a total blank. But then, suddenly, a rumor flew into our homeroom like a giant horsefly, buzzing around from desk to desk. Billy Beezer had gotten into trouble with the police the previous evening at the Bay View Mall. He was being charged with petty larceny, or shoplifting in the third degree, or juvenile hoodlumism, or some such minor first offense. Our school has a policy: anyone who gets into trouble with the police and is charged with a crime is suspended for one week.

It's automatic.

Hence no Billy Beezer in school today. Or tomorrow. Or Friday, for that matter.

Also, according to the rumor, Billy Beezer's parents had grounded him for a month. So he would not be hanging out at the Bay View Mall anymore. Nor would he be able to attend after-school basketball games.

And suddenly I knew what I would do.

Right there, in homeroom, I ripped a piece of paper from my yellow notepad. My black ball-point pen shook slightly in my trembling right hand as I wrote out the fateful question: "Gloria, will you go to the basketball game with me this Friday?" Beneath that monumental question, I drew two boxes. One box was conspicuously large. I labeled it the YES box. The second box was tiny. I labeled it the NO box.

And that is the yellow piece of paper I have folded up into a square and am holding in my damp hand as I wait here on Torture Island for Mrs. Moonface to turn toward the blackboard and give me the opportunity I need.

I cannot approach Glory Hallelujah after class because she is always surrounded by her friends. I cannot wait and pass the note to her later in the week because she may make plans to go to the game with one of her girlfriends. No, it is very evident to me that today is the day, and that I must pass the note before this period ends or forever live a coward.

There are only ten minutes left in this anti-math class. Mrs. Moonface seems to have no intention of recording her algebraic observations for posterity. Perhaps the piece of yellow chalk in her hand is just a prop. It is possible that the previous night she hurt her wrist in an arm-wrestling competition and can no longer write. It is also possible that she has forgotten all about her students and believes that she is playing a part in a Hollywood movie.

Mrs. Moonface, I am sorry, but this is not *Gone With the Wind* and you are not Vivien Leigh. This is not even *Gone With a Faint Breeze*. This is anti-math class and you are our teacher, and even though I can't hear a word you're saying because I am marooned on Torture Island, I would like to remind you that your other students need to record the exact nature of your valuable algebraic theorizing. To do this, they need visual assistance. So write something down!

There are only seven minutes left in anti-math class. I attempt to turn Mrs. Moonface toward the blackboard by telekinesis. The atoms of her body prove remarkably resistant to my telepathic powers.

There are six minutes left. Now there are five.

Mrs. Moonface, for Pete's sake, write something on the blackboard! That is what mathematics teachers do! Write down axioms, simplify equations, draw rectangles, measure angles, even, if you must, sketch the sneering razor-toothed face of Algebra itself.

Suddenly Mrs. Moonface stops lecturing. Of course, I cannot hear her, because no sound penetrates the isolation of Torture Island, but I can see her mouth stop moving. Her right hand, holding the chalk, rises.

Then her hips begin to pivot.

This all unfolds in very slow motion. The sheer importance of the moment slows the action way, way down.

The pivoting of Mrs. Moonface's hips causes a corresponding rotation in the plane of her shoulders and upper torso.

Her neck follows her shoulders, as day follows night.

Eventually, the lunar surface of her face is pulled toward the blackboard.

She begins to write. I have no idea what she is writing. It could be hieroglyphics and I would not notice. It could be a map to Blackbeard's treasure and I would not care.

I am now primed. My heart is thumping against my ribs, one by one, like a hammer pounding out a musical scale on a metal keyboard. Bing. Bang.

Bong. Bam. I am breathing so quickly that I cannot breathe, if that makes any sense. I must be moving off Torture Island because I can now hear every sound in the room. My peripheral vision has increased sevenfold. I believe that one of my eyes has actually slid across my face and now sits, flounder-like, atop my head.

I am aware of every single one of my classmates in anti-math class. I can see that, in a corner of the room, Karen Direggio, who I have rather cruelly nicknamed Dirigible on account of a slight weight problem and the fact that she is full of hot air, is copying formulas furiously into her notebook. And I can see that Norman Cohen, who sits to the right of Glory Hallelujah and who I have rechristened Norman Cough because of a chronic bronchial problem he has had since the fifth grade, to which the Centers for Disease Control should definitely be paying more attention, is also writing furiously.

In short, everyone in anti-math class is now preoccupied. There are only four minutes left in the period. Mrs. Moonface is filling up blackboard space at an unprecedented clip, no doubt trying to scrape every last kernel of anti-mathematical knowledge from the corncob of her brain before the bell. My classmates are racing to keep up with her. All around me pens are moving across notebooks at such a rate that ink can barely leak out and affix itself to paper.

The confluence of rapid writing on the part of Mrs. Moonface and speed-copying on the part of my classmates has created the exact double void in space and time that I need to accomplish my mission!

My moment is at hand! The great clapper in the bell of fate clangs for me! *Ka-wang! Ka-wang!*

My heart escapes from the cage of my ribs, swims valiantly up my aorta and into my carotid artery like a salmon heading for its ancestral breeding ground, somehow vaults the blood barrier to my brain, pushes the main switchboard operator who normally sits there and is a notorious coward out of his swivel chair, and begins pulling levers.

My right hand rises and begins to move sideways, very slowly, like a submarine, traveling at sub-desk depth to avoid teacher radar.

My right index finger makes contact with the sacred warm left wrist of Glory Hallelujah!

She looks down to see who is touching her at sub-desk depth. Spots my hand, with its precious yellow note.

Gloria understands instantly.

The exchange of the covert note is completed in a nano-instant. Mrs. Moonface and the rest of our anti-math class have no idea that anything momentous has taken place.

I reverse the speed and direction of my right hand, and it returns safely to port.

Meanwhile, my eye—the one that has become mobile—slips down from the top of my head and finds a spot behind my right ear, which affords it a perfect view of Glory Hallelujah.

She has transferred my note to her lap and has moved her right elbow to block anyone on that side of her from seeing. The desk itself provides added shielding.

In the clever safe haven that she has created, she unfolds my note. Reads it.

Time is suddenly standing still. Literally. The sweeping second hand of our classroom's clock is frozen at the seven.

I am watching Glory Hallelujah for the slightest hint of a reaction, which will also serve as an answer.

She does not need to speak. She does not need to check the YES or NO boxes on my note. If she merely blinks, I will understand. If she wrinkles her nose, the import of her nose wrinkle will not be lost on me. In fact, so total is my concentration in that moment of grand suspense I am absolutely positive that there is nothing that Glory Hallelujah can do, no reaction that she can give off, that I will not immediately and fully understand.

I would stake my life on it.

But what she does do is this. She folds my note back up. Without looking at me—without even an eye blink or a nose wrinkle—she raises it to her lips. For one wild instant I think that she is going to kiss it. But then her lovely lips, like twin rosebud petals in spring sunlight, spread themselves open.

Her pearly teeth part.

She eats my note.

I am happy to report that no chewing is involved. She swallows it in one gulp, like a vitamin C tablet. I watch my note slide the length of her delicate esophagus.

She still has not looked at me.

The bell rings. The double void of space and time

is fractured irreparably. Everyone suddenly stands and begins packing up books. Glory Hallelujah's friends surround her, and she is swept out of the classroom without a backward glance.

My deepest secret is now lodged, quite literally, inside of her.

permit me a father fantasy

Here is my problem in a nutshell: polite requests for Friday night dates can be accepted or rejected, laughed at or cried over, but I believe, even with my limited experience, that they are very rarely ingested. I am having a difficult time working out the thought processes that could have led Glory Hallelujah to eat my note.

All day in anti-school, I attempted to figure out what she could have been thinking as she was swallowing. Twice as classes changed I encountered Glory Hallelujah in hallways, but she was always surrounded by friends. I had no opportunity to approach her privately and ask for an explanation. Nor did she speak to me. In fact, though I may be paranoid, Glory Hallelujah appeared to turn her head away from me when we passed each other.

So I am trying to figure out her strange note-eating

behavior on my own. I have drawn up a list of possible explanations. It is now well past midnight, and while my list is not very long, I believe that I have made all the reasonable inductions, deductions, and just plain ductions that anyone could possibly draw to explain such a reaction to being asked out on a date.

I am the only one awake in my whole house. I have been working on my list, in bed, since exactly eleven minutes after eleven, when the man who is not my father pulled closed the door to the big bedroom down the hall—the room that is no longer my parents' room, and never will be again.

Permit me a father fantasy. It is odd, but I think I have never missed the man who named me after a toilet as much as I do on this night. I'm sure if he were here, instead of the brutish, snoring, pillow-bellied lout who is now sleeping next to my mother, he could explain Glory Hallelujah's behavior to me in five seconds flat.

Here is my father fantasy. The man who named me after a toilet has come home. He has returned with a perfectly logical explanation for disappearing for nearly a decade. "I was beamed aboard a UFO, son.

There was nothing I could do. I wanted to drop you and Mom a postcard, or at least give you a call, but they were hauling my ass all over the Milky Way. Took me nine years to get away and make my way back to you, but here I am now, home, to stay."

In my father fantasy, the man who named me after a toilet is tall and handsome, but, oddly enough, he still manages to look just like me. He has an easy, generous laugh and moves with a confident, athletic grace. Watching him gives me a deep thrill— I tell myself that since I am his son, one day the laws of genetics predict that I will grow up very much like him.

We are at the park. It is Sunday morning. We are tossing a football back and forth. My father has just shown me the great male secret of how to throw a spiral. "There, son," he says, "you're now part of the fraternity of perfect-spiral throwers. You will now be picked first or second in every gym class you are ever in."

"Thanks, Dad," I say. "I always knew there was a secret, and that if somebody just showed me, I could do it as well as anyone."

"Damn straight, son. They're gonna be calling you

Bazooka Arm from now on. And if there's ever anything else I can help you with, now that I'm back home, you just come and ask me. The world is full of secret knowledge, son, that men have been salting away for centuries, and it's my job as your father to pass it on to you."

"Well, Dad," I say, "as a matter of fact, I do have a question for you. It's about girls."

My father grins. "A slightly more difficult subject than throwing the perfect spiral, son. But ask away."

"I gave a girl a note today in class. She's real pretty, Dad. In the note, I asked her out on a date."

"Good for you, son. Chip off the old block."

"And . . . well . . . Dad, she ate my note."

"Ate it, son?"

"Yes, Dad. In one big gulp. And I don't know what to make of that."

"Son," my father says, laying a paternal arm across my shoulders, "I'm very glad you asked me that. Because without proper guidance, you might come to think that the female mind is strange and mysterious, and that the behavior it generates is beyond your capacity to understand. But I can explain it all to you in five seconds so that it makes perfect sense. Let me tell you a story. Do you know what happened on the day I got down on my knees and asked your mother to marry me?"

"She accepted?"

"Not right away, son. First I had to present her with a ring. And do you know what she did when I held out that ring?"

"No, Dad."

"She ate it, son. She popped that ring into her mouth and swallowed it down like a cherry pit. And, I have to admit, her response might have confused me—might have ruined the entire damned experience—if I didn't know how to interpret it. But your grandfather understood such behavior, and he passed down the secret to me, so I was well prepared. And now, son, I will pass it on to you."

That is, unfortunately, as far as this particular father fantasy of mine goes. In a fantasy, I cannot have my father speak knowledge to me that I myself do not own. If I could complete this fantasy, I would not need to stay up late into the night making up a short list of explanations for Gloria's behavior, none of which I like very much.

Here are the possibilities as I see them.

First and most upsetting to me is the notion that perhaps Glory Hallelujah is not really a girl at all. It is true that she looks like a girl, acts like a girl, walks like a girl, and even gives off the perfumed aroma of a girl, but I have learned in my short life that things are not always what they seem. If my tuba can be a giant frog masquerading as a musical instrument, then it is possible that the girl of my dreams is actually not a girl at all but a hungry goat.

This makes a certain amount of logical sense. Please consider. If you pass a hungry goat a note, the goat will not nod or smile or check the YES or NO box and pass the note back. The goat will look upon your note not as a means of communication but, rather, as lunch.

Put in analogy form: a note to a goat is like a hot dog to a human.

I am having a hard time accepting this theory because it clashes so strongly with my own sensory observations. Glory Hallelujah is the girliest girl I have ever known. She is the essence of feminine, attractive girlness. Conversely, whatever that means, she is also the least goaty girl I have ever met. If she is indeed a goat pretending to be a girl, her disguise is truly magnificent.

Hypothesis two is my best-case scenario. Maybe she did not mean to eat my note. Perhaps Glory Hallelujah was raising her hand to her lips to kiss my note in a tender gesture.

It is conceivable that at the very second when she was raising my note for this completely understandable and delightful purpose, she was forced by some reflexive sneeze-squelching or belch-stifling mechanism to inhale suddenly and involuntarily through her mouth. My note became caught in the airstream and was sucked into her lungs, much as airport birds are occasionally sucked into jet engines.

This would explain why she did not try to talk to me for the rest of the day, and even seemed to look away when we passed each other in school hallways. Perhaps she is as embarrassed at having involuntarily eaten my note as I am mystified by her behavior. Mine may well be the first note she has ever accidentally eaten. She may not know how to explain herself.

The only problem with this theory is that I was watching Glory Hallelujah very carefully at the moment of note ingestion, and I saw no evidence of a sneeze or belch, even in its most formative stages. In fact, I believe that she was respiring quite normally.

I myself stifle a yawn with my right hand. It is now nearing one in the morning. I am sitting up in bed in my tiny bedroom that is not a bedroom, working on my short list by pencil flashlight beam.

The reason I must use a small flashlight is that if the man who is not my father caught me up this late, there would be hell to pay. "What's this?" he would bellow, kicking my door wide open. "What have we here?" he would demand, yanking the covers off my bed. "Another dirty magazine, is it? Having fun with yourself again, are you? You disgusting filthy pervert."

The man who is not my father is not a great believer in personal privacy, at least when I am involved. He has surprised me late at night several times. On the slightest pretext, he will search my room. The only incriminating thing he has ever found was an issue of *National Geographic*, which contained an article on an Amazon tribe who—no doubt because they live in a sweltering jungle—do not wear many articles of clothing.

Now, let me stress, this was in no way pornography. This was an educational article in a respectable magazine, and the accompanying photographs were selected to make anthropological points. The reason

I was reading it in my bed, late at night, was because I could not sleep. And the reason I happened to be studying a photograph of a teenage girl with bare breasts was because at the moment when the man who is not my father burst in on me, I had just turned the page.

The man who is not my father carried my magazine down the hall to show my mother, shouting in a voice loud enough to be heard in Hong Kong, "Look what that filthy little pervert was getting his jollies with! Tried to hide it under the bed when I came in."

I stood in the doorway to the hall, nearly paralyzed by anger and shame, and listened to her response.

"Oh, he's just a growing boy, Stan. Let him be, and let's all get some sleep. Weren't you a boy once?"

"Not like that, thank God. Filthy little pervert."

Luckily, on this night, I can hear the man who is not my father snoring away in the big bedroom at the end of the hall. I would call it my parents' bedroom, but since he sleeps there, and he is not in any way a parent to me, and never will be, I will describe the room merely by its size and location.

I can hear him snoring in short, loud bursts, like a man cutting evenly sized pieces of firewood with a chain saw. He wears boxer shorts to bed, and his big hairy stomach hangs out over the elastic band of his shorts like a kangaroo pup trying to climb out of its mother's pouch.

My mother is sleeping next to him. It is amazing that anyone can sleep with such a racket going on. But my mother worked a double shift at the factory today, and I believe that she could sleep through a cavalry charge.

Of course, if I felt really desperate, and also masochistic, whatever that means, I could ask the man who is not my father to explain Gloria's behavior to me. I can just imagine what he would say. "Ate it, did she? Hah!" He would burst into laughter. "Serves you right, you little weirdo."

"But why did she eat it?"

"Because she despises you," the man who is not my father would say. "So much so that she thinks you should end up in a toilet." He can be very vulgar, this man my mother has chosen from among the approximately two billion other candidates on earth.

But I must admit there is a part of me that thinks he would not be completely wrong in his analysis. My third and last attempt to explain Glory Hallelujah's behavior is extremely distressing. It is possible that Gloria does not share my unbounded feelings of admiration and affection.

In my enthusiasm and inexperience, I may have misread the road signs. Instead of SPEED UP the signs may have said SLOW DOWN, CLIFF AHEAD. It may go beyond the fact that she may not like me. She may find me unpleasant in a wide variety of ways that I do not like to think about.

Following this line of logic to its grisly conclusion, perhaps Glory Hallelujah found my request for a date so horrific, so totally revolting, and so beyond the bounds of acceptable social interchange, given our relative popularity at our anti-school, that she had to destroy it immediately.

It wasn't enough for her to decline my offer by shaking her head side to side, or checking the NO box on the note, or even by ripping my note into small pieces. She needed to completely and utterly negate it.

By eating my note, she effectively obliterated its existence in time and space. She may have been saying to me, "You have no right to put me in the position of having to consider going on a date with you. So I am going to make your request vanish."

This third and last theory is unpleasant to contemplate, but it does seem to have the ring of truth. Its major weakness is that it is hard for me to believe that Glory Hallelujah could dislike me so much, and that a girl with the face of an angel could ever be so cruel.

She must know how I feel about her. We have exchanged telepathic messages for months. We have passed each other the secret signals of the hair brushback and the ear scratch.

Surely she understands that my passing her the note was not an easy thing for me to do, and that I am basically a good person, with a good heart, which beats for her and her alone.

But then there is another possibility that gives me pause.

It is possible that—like you, like Mr. Steenwilly, like everyone else in my life that is not really a life— Glory Hallelujah does not know me.

She may, in fact, not know me at all.

9

the happiest day of my life

The happiest day of my life begins unhappily. I wake up late, from a sleep that is not a sleep. It cannot be a real sleep because when I wake up, I am exhausted. In fact, I am far more tired than I was at three in the morning when I put away my list and my pencil flashlight and closed my eyes.

I do not understand how sleep can make me tired. Sometimes I suspect that while my mind thinks it is asleep I have actually been transported to an alternate universe where I was forced to run laps all night, or to march with alien armies over rough terrain.

I also wake up afraid. The fear increases as I get out of bed and begin pulling on clothes. I barely manage to hide the growing dread as I sit at our table that is not a table dredging up soggy flakes of cereal.

I am afraid because I have no doubt that in some

way or other Glory Hallelujah will respond to my note today, and I fear the worst.

Last night, while I was making up my list to try to figure out her behavior, she was probably telling all her friends about my note. Perhaps there was a mass meeting of the secret sorority of pretty fourteen-year-old girls, and Glory Hallelujah stepped forward. "Sisters," she said, "you won't believe what happened to me this morning in anti-math class. I was passed a note so stupid and pathetic that I had to eat it. And here is what the note said. And you'll never believe who had the nerve to give it to me."

I am afraid as I walk to school. Every time I see a member of the secret sorority of pretty fourteen-year-old girls I look the other way.

I walk past Billy Beezer's house and see no sign of him. Besides his being suspended and grounded, it would not surprise me if Mr. and Mrs. Beezer have also chained him up in the basement. They have high hopes for their young Beezer. They believe that he will graduate first in his class from our anti-school, go to Harvard, become President, and also discover a cure for old age.

They cannot have been too thrilled about his egg-roll-stealing caper. I believe that the full wrath of the disappointed Beezer parents has descended on my friend who is not a friend. I look for his face in the window, but the curtains have all been pulled closed as if out of a deep sense of shame.

I arrive at school two minutes early. My locker is on the third floor, in a fairly remote corner. I turn the dial on the combination lock three to the left, four to the right, five to the left, but there are no hopeful clicks and the door remains sealed tight. This does not surprise me. My locker does not work the way other lockers do. It is not at all impressed by correct combinations. My locker is far tougher and meaner than that.

I do not dial the combination again right away. "Open up," I whisper. "I am in no mood for this today. If you give me trouble, you will regret it."

My locker does not respond, because it has no mouth, but what it is thinking is "Take your best shot, doofus. My grandfather was a vault at Fort Knox and I don't open for the likes of you."

I kick my locker so hard that I dent it. It is possible that I also fracture several of my toes. I begin to hop around in pain. And then I lower my injured foot and the pain vanishes because I see Glory Hallelujah herself in all her glory walking toward me, and she looks relatively happy, although she appears slightly baffled at something she has just seen. "Are you okay?" she asks.

"Oh, yes," I say, suddenly dizzy as the full force of her bright blue eyes is turned in my direction. Forgive me for being dramatic, but it is like standing on a high hill, looking into a sunrise. "Fine," I gasp, "just fine."

"You kicked your locker."

"Just practicing a soccer move."

"I didn't know you play soccer," she says.

"I play all sports," I tell her. And then, because I have been rendered giddy by looking into the mountain sunrise of her blue eyes, I am able to blurt out, "Why did you eat my note?"

She smiles. The lights of the universe blink on and off. Matter and antimatter nearly come together. She is smiling at me. *At me!* "I was hungry," she says.

So she is a goat. Well, no matter. Goat or girl, she is still my beloved. Her secret is safe with me. I will bring her pieces of paper and tin cans. I will tie a bell around her neck and lead her to green and grassy pastures.

"That was a joke, silly," she says. "What else was I going to do with your note? I mean, you passed it to me right at the end of class. Mrs. Gabriel was about to turn around and catch us. I couldn't risk having her find it."

I am smiling back at her, and nodding at her response, and I am thinking, "Of course. It makes perfect sense. Eat the evidence. If Billy Beezer had swallowed the egg roll, he could have denied everything. He would be a free man now."

"And I was a little bit surprised," she says. "I didn't know you even liked me."

"Well . . ." I start to say, and run out of words.

"I mean, I kind of thought so. But you never said anything."

"But . . ." I try to point out, and don't know how to finish the sentence.

"I thought maybe you might say something to me after math class yesterday, but every time I saw you after that, it seemed like you were embarrassed, and hurried away."

"No . . ." I try to explain, but how can I begin to describe such a complex case of mutual misunderstanding?

Glory Hallelujah is watching me. "I guess you're a little shy," she says. "Is that it?"

I nod.

"Shy is good," she says. "I have a horse, Luke. Well, actually I just own half of Luke. Isn't that weird, to just own half a horse? Anyway, Luke is real shy. If he doesn't know you, he won't take an apple from your hand. Even if he's hungry. But once he gets to know you, he's the friendliest horse in the whole world."

I am trying to follow all this, but I am still a bit dizzy and the words are flying thick and fast. I know that I am being compared to half a horse. Usually this would not be a good thing, but in this case it sounds just fine. I am quite willing to be either the front or even the back half of a horse if Glory Hallelujah thinks I am the friendliest horse in the world. I would eat an apple out of her hand. I would eat a pineapple from the crook of her elbow. If necessary, I believe I would be willing to eat a guava, skin and all, from between her feet.

The bell rings. We have to be in homeroom in three minutes.

"Oops, I better go get my books," Glory Hallelujah says, and takes a step away.

I am surprised to hear myself say, "Wait a minute, Gloria."

She turns. Waits.

My heart is going *Ka-wang! Ka-wang!* "Do you want to come to the game with me or not?"

Once again, I feel the intensity of her friendly smile. Not to be overly poetic, but I believe it is akin to the shaft of heavenly light the shivering polar explorer sees that cracks apart the treacherous ice floe, and opens a safe route home. "Of course I do, John," she says. It is the first time she has ever spoken my name. I did not know until this very instant that she even knew my name. But apparently she does. Because her lips have just uttered it, more musically than it has ever been spoken before. "I love basketball. And I think we should get to know each other better. Do you mind picking me up at home?"

"No," I say.

"You know where I live? Beechwood Lane, all the way down at the end."

"Sure," I say. I am thinking: "Of course I know where you live. There is nothing about you I don't know, Glory Hallelujah! I know the different pairs of your white and yellow and pink socks, and how high they stretch up your delicate ankles, which you are in the habit of crossing and uncrossing beneath your chair during anti-math class. I have counted the tiny blond hairs on the side of your ear, and I am also intimately familiar with the pattern of freckles on your left elbow."

"And do you think we should get something to eat after the game? Maybe at the Center Street Diner?"

"Absolutely," I say, and hear myself babble, "Dinner. Diner. Done!"

"Great. See you in math class," she says. "Bye, John."

She walks away down the corridor. I turn to my locker. Dial three to the left, four to the right, five to the left. The door swings open.

My locker is now aware that it is dealing with someone who can't be messed with. It has listened to my entire conversation with Glory Hallelujah, and it has seen that I am a player. It knows that if it gives me trouble I can have its door removed from its hinges, melted down, and reshaped at a foundry into gardening tools or toilet paper holders.

My locker practically places the correct textbooks in my hands. It does not have a mouth, so it cannot speak, but my locker is thinking, "I did not know who I was dealing with. You were traveling through this school incognito. I mistook you for a doofus. But now I see who you really are, and it is a great honor to serve such a scholar and gentleman."

I close my locker door and head down the hall. Now, this is a very strange thing, but the school corridor itself looks markedly different. It takes me a few seconds to figure out what has changed. For the first time in my life, I am actually seeing the tops of the rows of lockers. Either I have grown a foot taller, or I am floating on air. It is also possible that the lockers themselves have shrunk.

Indeed, my entire anti-school and everyone in it seem to have decreased in size, relative to me. The doorways seem smaller. The water fountains seem lower. I pass several guys in football team jackets, standing and talking loudly, in a kind of pre-school huddle. They have a way of filling up the entire hallway with their squared shoulders, so that I normally have to squeeze by on the side or scamper and weave my way through them like a bug scuttling, terrified, across a kitchen floor, all the time saying, "Excuse me, pardon me." Today they don't look nearly so big in their silly white jackets. I saunter right through the midst of their huddle, like John Wayne through a saloon, brushing shoulders with them.

As homeroom period yields to first period, and then to second, I notice an even stranger thing. The school day is unfolding in real time. The mysterious and wrathful God of school clocks—who normally tortures me by slowing down each period of my anti-school day so that five minutes of anti-math class can take five hours—has vanished. All of the different hands of all of the different school clocks are turning at their correct speed. Teachers are teaching in real time. Students are studenting. Radiators are radiating.

I am also noticing many attractive features of our anti-school that I have for some reason never observed before. One of the second-floor hall windows looks out on a corner of a grassy field, in the center of which a maple tree spreads its branches in a most picturesque fashion, as if it is embracing the sky. I also spot, hanging on the wall of our chemistry lab, next to the equipment closet, a small print of Robert Wilhelm Bunsen, which I have never noticed before. In this important work of portraiture, Dr.

Bunsen is shown holding up one of his Bunsen burners with obvious pride. It is, I'm sure you will agree, surprising how we are practically surrounded by beauty and great works of art, and yet oblivious to them.

Good old Mrs. Moonface is waiting for us at the front of anti-math class, ready to spout algebraic gibberish as always. She gives me a perplexed look, because I am always the very last one to squeeze into the room just as she is starting her lecture, and today I am two minutes and twenty-seven seconds early.

I return her perplexed look with a nonchalant nod of the head—one might even say a fearless nod of the head. "Yes, I have come early and of my own free will, Mrs. Moonface. What is more, I refuse the blindfold. Line me up against the wall and fire away with your most deadly algebra. I have arrived with a smile on my face, and if I must die, it will be with the same brave smile. For I will see the face of my beloved before I expire."

I sit down at my desk. Mrs. Moonface is still throwing me perplexed looks. She can tell that something has changed. She can see that I have lost my fear of algebra. On this day, I have more important matters on my mind than any concept in the entire history of mathematics. I am waiting for Glory Hallelujah—*my* Glory Hallelujah—to arrive.

Believe me, if Archimedes ever had the grand entrance of a girl as pretty as Gloria to look forward to, he would never have spent so much time calculating the value of pi. He would have been baking her a pie! If Euclid had ever beheld a vision of loveliness like the one I see walking into my anti-math class, he would have forgotten all the geometry of lines and planes, and concentrated on the sweet simplicity of soft curves. If Pythagoras had ever had a girl look at him the way Gloria's blue eyes fix in my direction, he would have given up his calculations on the hypotenuse of right triangles and run for the hills to pick a bouquet of wildflowers.

Yes, that's right, Gloria walks into anti-math class and looks right at me, and gives me a little smile. She passes in front of a bank of windows and is backlit by a heavenly radiance. The lovely lines of her long legs and perfect thighs are gilded, as if by a worshipful artist, by the noon sunlight. Her perky breasts press against her T-shirt as if reaching out to greet me through the flimsy cotton material. With each step her hips swivel and she seems to toss her head slightly, so that her golden hair glitters.

Among the Lashasa Palulu, there is no word for God. When speaking of divine things, they merely point at the sun. When they are indoors, they must do this with their feet, since they walk on their hands. If you have never seen a group of Lashasa Palulu praying indoors, with their toes pointed skyward, you have missed something. As Glory Hallelujah enters my anti-math class and smiles at me, I am tempted to spring onto my hands and point my feet skyward in a prayer of thanks, but I restrain myself.

Then we are sitting side by side, sharing the delicious secret of our Friday night date. I know she is thinking about it, even though she manages—no doubt through a huge effort of will—to give no outward sign that anything unusual has taken place between us. She appears to be listening carefully to Mrs. Moonface, but she is, of course, thinking of what our life will be like together, henceforth.

I am also pretending to listen to Mrs. Moonface. I have long ago perfected the technique—invaluable in anti-math class—of not being noticed by being noticed. Let me explain.

I hold this truth to be self-evident: No one wants to be called on to answer a question in algebra class. Everyone in our class is, in effect, trying to hide in their seat. Some are using camouflage—dressing to blend in with the walls. Some are attempting to throw her off with the old blank poker face or the old dead-fish gaze, as if to say, "Don't bother calling on me, Mrs. Moonface, because I am brain-dead."

Others are using the more advanced but equally foolhardy technique of trying to appear eager, smiling and copying down her lecture enthusiastically, as if to say, "There's no need to call on me, Mrs. Moonface, because I'm right with you."

I have combined elements from all of these approaches to arrive at the one, true method of not being noticed by being noticed. This highly sophisticated technique for not getting called on involves just enough head movement, facial expression, and note-taking enthusiasm so that Mrs. Moonface will not think I am trying to hide from her, combined with just enough of a blank poker face and a dead-fish gaze so that she will also not think I am trying to trick her by appearing overeager.

So I am now sitting at my desk, watching her teach

and thinking about my date with Glory Hallelujah. Of course, I do not understand the slightest syllable of algebra gibberish that Mrs. Moonface is uttering, but she cannot tell that from my appearance.

I am applying my technique with masterly precision. After every second sentence from Mrs. Moonface I nod my head, each time she finishes writing down an equation I move my pencil as if jotting down a few key ideas, and twice every three minutes I meet her eyes and smile knowingly, while at the same time allowing the slightest spark of understanding to creep into my dead-fish gaze.

My technique is working perfectly. I am invisible. When she turns from the board and does her quick death scan to decide who will fail at answering her next impossible question, there is nothing about me to trigger the slightest firing of neurons in her brain. Her death scan sweeps on, past me, past Karen Dirigible, who has dressed so perfectly to blend in with the walls that I myself cannot distinguish girl from painted plaster, to Norman Cough, who attempts to deflect it with a pathetic retching sound from his bronchial repertoire, as if to say, "Don't call on me—can't you see that I'm dying of tuberculosis?"

"Norman," Mrs. Moonface says, "I'd like to ask you to answer this very simple problem," and she taps the chalk on the board for emphasis. "An automobile radiator contains 20 quarts of a 40 percent antifreeze solution. How many quarts should be drained and replaced with pure antifreeze if the final mixture is to be 50 percent antifreeze?"

Norman squints his eyes and makes a face like there is antifreeze rolling around in his eyeballs. He looks at us, his classmates, for help, but we have seen him get the death question and are all looking away from him, as if he has just been diagnosed with leprosy. He looks back at Mrs. Moonface for mercy, with eyes that are as big and panicked and pleading as a deer's suddenly caught in a sixteen-wheeler's headlights. "Please," Norman's eyes are begging, "I have a miserable enough life as it is, merely being Norman Cough. There is no need to humiliate me with this algebra question from the lowest level of hell. I stand less chance of answering it than I do of levitating myself out the window. I humbly beg of you, Mrs. Moonface, as one human being to another, in accordance with the United Nations Charter and the Geneva Convention, withdraw your question."

Mrs. Moonface smiles back at him. But the message buried in her smile is: "Norman, you are dead meat. Since I will never be a movie star and get my own trailer and have a sandwich tray delivered every hour by a handsome man named Jacques, I have declared war against the entire human race, and the most potent weapon in my arsenal is the unanswerable mixture equation question. You have been selected from all of the students in this anti-math class by my random death scan to be destroyed and forever branded a doofus by this particular question. There is no way out. Abandon hope." But what Mrs. Moonface actually says is: "Norman, we're waiting for your answer."

Norman realizes that he is trapped. There are animals that nature has provided with multiple weapons and defenses. The flying squirrel, for example, has sharp teeth and claws, a bristly coat, and a membrane that enables it to glide through the air. But there are also less sophisticated life forms that, when tracked by a predator, have one and only one trick to try to escape. There are, for example, worms that roll themselves into tight balls, and squid that squirt black clouds of ink to try to blind their attackers. Norman

Cough is such a one-trick organism. Nature has furnished him with only a single defensive weapon to try to survive in the battle of evolution—a repulsive hacking cough.

Norman tilts his jaw, opens his mouth to a circumference that seems somehow wider than the total girth of his head, and tries to cough his way out of his dilemma with a throat-rattling tonsil-grinding explosion unlike any I have ever heard before. The soles of my feet actually feel the floor of our classroom vibrate.

But Mrs. Moonface is not impressed. I believe that the trumpet blast that shook down the walls of Jericho would not prevent her from demanding an answer to her antifreeze question. "Norman, I'm waiting for an answer and I'm running out of patience. I'm going to count to three."

At this moment, a very strange thing happens. A most remarkable occurrence takes place. In my attempt to avoid making eye contact with the doomed, I have been looking away from Norman. At first I gazed on the lovely form of Glory Hallelujah, but lest she feel like I am staring at her, my eyes drift past her lovely countenance and, for lack of anything else to fix on, gaze blankly at the algebraic nonsense that Mrs. Moonface has written on the blackboard.

I am not thinking about antifreeze and mixture equations. I am thinking about Friday night, and what it will be like to pick Gloria up at her house, and how it will feel to take her soft hand in my own when we cross busy intersections. Suddenly I find that I am not only looking at the equations on the blackboard but actually understanding several of them. And then, to my horror, I find my right arm beginning to rise.

I try to clamp it to my side. It disobeys. With a supreme effort of will, I manage to halt its progress for several seconds, but then it breaks free and begins to rise again of its own accord. "Down, boy," I hiss, "get down," but my arm is already at a dangerously exposed angle, and soon, despite my very best efforts, my right hand is pointing toward the ceiling.

Mrs. Moonface sees my arm go up, but she ignores it because she knows that I cannot possibly have a contribution to make in this anti-math class. "Norman," she says, "I'm losing patience." But what she is really saying to him is: "A big fat 'F' for class participation in algebra is about five seconds away, and there is nothing you can do about it."

While she torments Norman, Mrs. Moonface is giving me valuable time to recover, but I simply cannot get control of my rebellious limb. In desperation, I attempt to make a deal with my right arm. "Lower yourself, and I will buy shirts with lovely long sleeves. Lower yourself, and I will always sleep on my left side, so the weight of my body never rolls over on you."

But not only does my right arm not accept the bribe—it actually begins to wave back and forth. Even Mrs. Moonface cannot ignore this. "John," she says, "you may go to the rest room."

I attempt to rise and exit, but to my shock my knees have taken up the rebellion. They do not swing out from under the desk and rise. Instead, my lips open and I hear my voice saying, "Thank you, Mrs. Gabriel, but I do not need to use the bathroom."

"Then what do you want?" she asks, annoyed.

"I wish to make a mathematical observation."

There are some laughs in the back of the class.

"Is this some kind of joke?" Mrs. Moonface asks.

I am fighting a losing battle to lock my lips and keep my vocal cords from twitching. My entire body is now in open rebellion. "No," I hear myself say. "It's just that Norman cannot possibly answer your question."

"Oh? And why is that?"

"Because I believe you have made a calculation mistake in one of the examples you have given us." The room has now gone completely silent. "Specifically, in example two, the third line of the solution. The two sides of the equation do not add up equally. No doubt this error is the source of Norman's confusion."

Norman makes a noncommittal sound deep in his throat. What he is saying is: "If you are right, and you save me from this antifreeze problem, I will follow you around for the rest of your life on my knees, knocking my head to the pavement at suitable intervals, but if you are wrong, prepare to meet your maker."

Mrs. Moonface's face turns so pale that I believe all the blood in her body has drained down to her big toe. "I don't think I made a mistake," she says, her eyes narrowing. "But let me check." She turns back to the blackboard. Seconds tick by. The classroom is totally silent, except for Norman Cough's deep, frightened breaths. Finally, slowly, she half turns back to face us and says, "Yes, yes, you're right, there is a mistake. Thank you, John, for catching it."

As she corrects the mistake, I hear something I have never heard before. It sounds like a breeze whistling around in the corners of the room. It takes me a second to realize what it is. Applause. My class-mates are clapping for me.

Mrs. Moonface repairs her error. She turns back to us, breathing fire. "There, I have fixed the example, and now, Norman, why don't you answer the antifreeze problem?"

But, just as the word "problem" escapes from her lips, the bell rings signaling the end of the period. "I would like to," Norman tells her, "but I have to go to my next class now. I don't want to be late. Sorry. Maybe next time." And so saying, Norman gathers up his books and exits the classroom at the speed of light.

We all follow him out. I myself exit behind Glory Hallelujah, who gives me an admiring smile. The applause is still ringing in my ears as I smile back.

10

the best day of my life
gets better

I am sitting in band practice, holding on to my tuba that is not a tuba, thinking that glee felt good for as long as it lasted. I sense I am in deep trouble now.

Not just because the giant frog who is posing as my tuba is in an unusually lethargic mood, whatever that means. He is either asleep or dead. Not just because we are about to get a new piece of music, which I will presumably not be able to play at all, since I have never been able to play any of the old pieces of music.

I surmise that I am in deep trouble because Mr. Steenwilly keeps looking at me.

Mr. Steenwilly, surely there are other directions you can direct that rather piercing gaze of yours. Surely your mustache can quiver at another member of our band family. Now that you have mounted that silly wooden podium in front of the band, from which you conduct, I suggest you turn your attention to Violent Hayes, who has succeeded in establishing what I believe in professional wrestling circles is termed a Mongolian death lock on the monitor lizard that is posing as her saxophone.

Mr. Steenwilly, why are you not starting to conduct? Why do you not wave your arms around and conjure music from silence? Why are you smiling and clearing your throat, and stealing one last look at me?

"It is time," Mr. Steenwilly announces grandly, as if making a proclamation of biblical magnitude, "for a new piece of music by Arthur Flemingham Steenwilly." He pulls a sheaf of papers out of a leather folio, hesitates, and then lowers his voice to a near whisper. "It's not for me to say it, my friends and students, but I think this is my best work, and may well be what I am remembered for in years to come. I am proudest of the tuba solo, which I expect John to make shimmy and shine like an April rainbow."

There are audible laughs from several of the less polite members of our band family. Unfortunately, I must agree with these skeptics.

Mr. Steenwilly, I am very sorry, but I do not believe there will be any April rainbows today in our band room. There may be a November sleet storm, but that is as close as I am likely to come. Why don't you just get it over with and call the music police, and cart me away to the band gallows. "Guilty," the high music judge will say, "of murdering each and every note in the Steenwilly masterpiece. String him up."

But the music police do not arrive to cart me away in their van. Instead, I find myself flexing my fingers in some improvised and ridiculous fashion, as if I am warming up for a new Olympic event in competitive origami. The giant frog in my arms is slumbering peacefully and evinces no signs whatsoever of life. I believe that he has sunk to the bottom of whatever pond he thinks he lives in, and has entered some sort of hibernatory state.

Mr. Steenwilly begins distributing the different musical parts to the different band sections, and when he hands mine to me, he winks, his mustache quivers, and he whispers, "Do me proud, John."

I am afraid to look at this piece of music. But I am also aware that it is pointless even to try to play music without actually looking at the notes. So, with trembling hands, I turn Mr. Steenwilly's masterpiece toward me and scan it. At first glance, it seems to be written in ancient Chinese ideographs. Mr. Steenwilly, you must have handed me the wrong manuscript. This appears to be a treatise on rice farming compiled by the eighth-century Shao Lin monk Ling Han.

I turn the paper on its head, and see that I am mistaken. It was not written by a Shao Lin monk. It is, in fact, a musical composition. I vaguely recognize several obscure musical symbols, and there are also several dozen notes that seem to be jumping about the page like fleas on a dog, playing hide-and-seek amid the musical bars.

Mr. Steenwilly, the notes in my solo will not stay still, so I cannot read them. It follows, as day follows night, that if I cannot read them, I cannot possibly play them. Therefore, Mr. Steenwilly, I suggest you cancel band practice today, go into your office, and have a nice snooze.

Mr. Steenwilly, you are not listening to my suggestion. You are climbing onto your podium. You are raising your baton. Your eyes are flashing like those of a man who expects his genius to be revealed to the world at any second. In your mind you are thinking, there was Mozart, there was Beethoven, there was

Brahms, and now there will be Steenwilly! Your mustache is quivering with anticipation.

Down comes your arm, starting the piece. Violent Hayes attempts to play the opening interlude, but the monitor lizard that is pretending to be her saxophone has other ideas. It frees itself from her Mongolian death lock with a swipe of its claws, opens its razor-toothed jaws, and lets loose with a reptilian shriek that I believe has not been heard on this earth since the Jurassic era.

The sonic burst of saurian screech that emanates from Violent Hayes's saxophone nearly knocks Mr. Steenwilly off his conducting podium. Suddenly, his glasses are askew, his hair mussed, his face flushed. He throws her a look, as if to say, "What you have just done to the opening interlude of my masterpiece is an insult not just to music, not just to art, but to every noble impulse in the human heart, and I am going to recommend that the music police roast you alive over hot coals."

Violent Hayes does not say anything back to Mr. Steenwilly because she has not seen his look; she is too busy trying to protect her jugular against the fangs of the monitor lizard. The lizard also does not reply to Mr. Steenwilly in words, but it does let loose with a furious *kee-waaa* that I believe is akin to the hunting call sounded by raptors when they've grounded a pterodactyl, and begun moving in for the kill.

I cannot feel any sympathy for Violent Hayes, because my own moment of reckoning is nearly at hand. The tuba solo is approaching, swimming toward me through the composition like a hungry giant octopus.

There is nothing in the known universe that can save me now. Our school has thick walls, so it is unlikely an alien spacecraft will be able to beam me up from this basement band room. Nor is our school likely to catch fire in the next seventeen seconds. Nor, I am sorry to report, are we in an earthquake zone. I am doomed.

I remember Mr. Steenwilly's advice that I should try to think of a musical composition as a kind of story. But what story, and how will this help? Desperate for any assistance, I look up the page to see what Mr. Steenwilly has titled this piece. I had not done this previously, out of fear that Mr. Steenwilly had continued his propensity to give his musical works preposterous titles. After "The Gambol of the Caribou" and "The War Cry of the Ostrich," I was afraid to see what part of nature he had drawn upon for his newest inspiration.

But now I look. Suddenly my whole body goes numb. I have always been confident that Mr. Steenwilly, like everyone else in my miserable life, does not know me at all. But perhaps he does know me a little bit. Or perhaps he is telepathic and invisible waves from my mind have been picked up by the satellite-dish receptor of his quivering mustache. However it came about, the name of Arthur Flemingham Steenwilly's masterpiece is "The Love Song of the Bullfrog."

As soon as I read this, I feel the giant frog that is pretending to be my tuba wake up and stretch. The start of my tuba solo is now only a few seconds away. Desperate, I try to turn "The Love Song of the Bullfrog" into a story.

"Once upon a time," I tell my tuba, "there was a lonely bullfrog who lived at the bottom of a pond, and nobody knew who he was. One day, a beautiful princess came to the pond and sat on a rock, and began to cry tears like pearls. The bullfrog swam up to her and asked why she was crying.

" 'I am actually not a princess,' she said, 'even though I walk like a princess, talk like a princess, and smell like a princess. I am actually a beautiful frog babe that a jealous witch has turned into a princess. As you may guess, it is no fun being a princess. It is much more fun to be a frog babe. But I can reverse the spell only if a handsome frog will kiss me.'

"The bullfrog jumped up onto a lily pad, from thence hopped to her shoulder, and kissed her on the right ear. Instantly, the princess morphed into the most beautiful frog babe in the history of ponds. She had glistening slimy skin, a long, bright red tongue, and great legs, fore and hind. When the bullfrog saw her, he opened his mouth and spontaneously began to croak a song to her . . ."

It is now time for me to begin my tuba solo. To my surprise, the giant frog who is pretending to be my tuba suddenly comes very much to life. Perhaps my story has gotten his amphibian juices flowing. He opens his mouth and lets loose with the deepest, richest, sexiest sound that has ever floated across a pond at dusk. The sound filters into our band room like a fog.

I am not playing my tuba. I am merely trying to

hang on. I see Mr. Steenwilly throwing me excited glances. His mustache appears to be whirling like a helicopter rotor. In fact, he is in danger of lifting off. Hang on to something, Mr. Steenwilly. Do not lift off. This hurricane or whatever it is will pass quickly.

In fact, my tuba solo is already half over. But suddenly the notes begin jumping around the page more and more swiftly. They are no longer like fleas on a dog. They are now like electrons during a lightning storm. I am forced to spice up my story, just to keep up with the crazed notes that Arthur Flemingham Steenwilly has written.

"When she heard the bullfrog's love song," I tell my tuba, "the frog babe hopped up onto a lily pad of her own, and began dancing a four-legged cancan, slowly stripping off her princess dress. Soon she was dancing in the buff, as only a frog babe can. The bullfrog watched her dance, with the sun glinting golden behind her, and his love song suddenly turned into a rock-and-roll number that woke up every pond animal right down to the old beaver snoring at the bottom of the dam!"

The giant frog pretending to be my tuba needs no

more coaxing. He begins doing what I believe is a frog version of the twist, thrusting out his pelvis like a young Elvis. I am hanging on to my tuba with both hands and one leg. Sounds are coming out of it that I have never heard before. "Calm down, boy," I tell it. "Chill. You'll rupture your throat." I enfold my tuba in my arms. The rock song slows down to a final chorus, and then one last, loving, guttural frog note.

And then silence.

The piece is over. I expect to hear applause for the second time in one day, but this time there is no clapping. Instead, several members of our band family are looking at me.

Is that a tear in your eye, Mr. Steenwilly? Is that another tear? Are you now clearing your throat? "Thank you," Mr. Steenwilly says. "That's all for today. But"—and suddenly he is looking right at me—"may I just say that it is a moving thing to hear a gifted young musician find his true sound. A great and moving thing. And"—his voice cracks—"that's all. I humbly thank you."

I put my tuba into its case. Andy Pearce comes up to me. "Hey, John, you really nailed that solo."

"Thank you," I say, modestly. "Actually, I don't

know how I got through it."

"You got through it by playing it," Andy says, in his inimitable logical fashion, whatever that means. And then he asks, "Have you heard about Billy?"

"Just that he was grounded."

"Well, there's good news. His parents are showing some mercy. They're letting him out for the Fremont game on Friday. Isn't that cool of them? You know what a big B-ball fan he is."

"Yes," I say, snapping my case closed, "I know."

"Why don't you come to the game with us?" he suggests.

"I can't," I tell him. "But I am going to the game. So I'll see you there."

Andy Pearce leaves, and several other members of the band come up and congratulate me. Of course, I am the soul of modesty, whatever that means.

I put my tuba case on its shelf. I am ready to head out.

But suddenly, unexpectedly, a shadow falls over me. I find my way blocked by Violent Hayes. I do not mean to be unkind, but she is a big girl. Tall. Big-boned. Wide in the shoulders. "John," she says. There is nothing musical about the way Violent

Hayes pronounces my name. She says it as if we are on a sports field and she is choosing me for her rugby team.

"Violet," I respond in kind.

"You got down with that solo," she says.

"Thank you," I say, and attempt to walk around her.

Somehow she manages to remain directly in front of me. "I mean you really got down. You were hot, John."

Violent Hayes, why are you looking at me this way? Why have your eyes suddenly gotten so big and bright? You are a nice girl, and not unattractive, and more than a match for a monitor lizard, which is impressive in its own way, but surely you must know that Glory Hallelujah is my beloved. "Thanks," I say. "Now I must head to chem lab."

This time I do manage to swerve around her, but then I feel something. A highly unusual sensation. Violent Hayes, did you just give me a friendly pat on the shoulder? Was it my imagination, or did your hand, after the innocent pat, slide all the way across the top of my neck, from right shoulder blade to left? Is it possible, Violent Hayes, that while running your hand across the back of my neck, you pivoted your wrist so that for a second your rather long fingernails raked lightly across my rather soft skin?

Good God, Violent Hayes, what are you thinking?

"See you soon, John," she says as I beat a hasty retreat.

"Sure. Thanks. Gotta run. Bye."

11

in the war zone

I am aware from the moment I return home from school on Friday to prepare for my big date that something is wrong. My dog, Sprocket, is hiding in the basement. He is whimpering, and he won't come out to greet me. I suspect that the man who is not my father has beaten him.

The man who is not my father is not around. There is an open bottle of Wild Turkey on the dining room table, and a glass next to it that still contains a few drops of foul-smelling whiskey. The man who is not my father does not drink often, but when he does, it makes him mean.

Our dining room is a mess. Sections of a newspaper and several magazines have been tossed onto the floor. A lamp has been knocked over, and the bulb is broken. A chair has also been kicked over onto its side. I do not know exactly what caused all this carnage, but I am glad the man who is not my father is gone.

His truck, which he parks in front of our house, is also gone. It is not clear exactly what the man who is not my father does with his truck to earn the little bit of money he seems to make from time to time. He calls it "short hauling." I confess I do not know what that means. But I am glad that on this particular afternoon he is away. I hope that this short haul is longer than usual.

It is strange that my mother is not home. On Fridays, she usually finishes at the factory early and gets home before me. But on this particular afternoon, there is no sign of her.

I take Sprocket some food, but he is crouched under the workbench in the basement and will not come out. I am sympathetic, but I do not have time to commiserate with him. This is my big night.

I leave the food for him and walk back upstairs. The whole house is deserted and quiet, except for occasional dog whimpers that float up eerily from below. My house is no longer a house—it has the empty, ominous feel of a war zone after a battle.

I attempt to focus on happy things.

This is a very big night in my life that is not a life.

I take a long, hot shower. I wash each and every part of my body twice. It is unlikely that Glory Hallelujah will have cause to smell certain hairy parts of my body at very close range, but it is not entirely out of the question. The man who is not my father has some aftershave called Sailors' Musk. I borrow a few drops. He will not miss them.

Smelling like a musky sailor, I attempt to dress for success. Since I have the world's smallest wardrobe, this is not a difficult task. I put on my one pair of gray corduroy pants and my one good green sweater, which my mother gave me as a Christmas present two years ago, and my tan jacket with the flannel lining. I am now as good-looking, clean-smelling, and well dressed as it is possible for me to be.

I look in the mirror. I am actually not myself anymore, which is not a bad thing. I am now cleverly disguised as the person I want Gloria to think of as me.

The telephone rings. I do not choose to answer it. It cannot possibly be good news. The message machine picks up, there is a beep, and then I hear a familiar voice. It is the voice of Billy Beezer, my friend who is not a friend. "I know you're there, John," he says. "Don't be a coward. Pick up the phone."

I hesitate for a few seconds and then pick up the phone. "I am not a coward," I say.

"No," he says, "but you are a rat and a thief. I heard through the grapevine about your date tonight. You stole my date idea."

"I saw Gloria first and liked her first," I remind him. "And did you or did you not say 'tough eggs' to me in the Bay View Mall?"

"It was my idea to ask her to a basketball game," he responds.

"Dating ideas are not private property," I tell him. "If you wanted to keep control of it, you should not have bragged about it. You really have no one to blame but yourself."

A strange sound comes over the telephone. It sounds like the grinding of gears on a Jeep going up one of the steeper slopes of Mount Everest, but I believe it is actually Billy Beezer gnashing his teeth together in a kind of frenzy. "What kind of friend would move in on a girl when his buddy was grounded and couldn't fight back?" he demands, his voice rising. "That's betrayal! That's stabbing in the back!"

I do not like his tone of voice. Nor do I appreciate being accused of dishonorable behavior by a convicted egg roll felon who saw nothing wrong with moving in on the girl of my dreams, when I clearly liked her first. "Did you or did you not tell me that all is fair in love and war?" I remind him. "Those are your very words."

"Then it's war?" he asks. "Is that what you want? Okay, then, I declare war on you! Let the hostilities begin. *I will annihilate you, you dirt bag!*"

I am not afraid of Billy Beezer. I move the telephone receiver a bit farther from my ear to prevent deafness. "Control yourself, Billy," I tell him. "Why don't you cook yourself up a nice snack? Maybe an egg roll."

More gnashing of teeth. "Is that supposed to be funny? We'll see what's funny soon enough. We'll see what's hilarious. We'll see who's laughing last."

"I would like to discuss this with you further, Billy, but, as you know, I have somewhere important to go tonight, and I must finish preparing for my big date. I do not mean to rub it in, but it sounds to me like you have not learned the necessary lessons from your recent punishment. Rather than threatening innocent people, I suggest you concentrate on becoming a better human being. Goodbye."

"It's not goodbye for long," Billy Beezer rumbles ominously. "I'm now ungrounded. I'll be there myself, tonight, at the Fremont game. Don't think you're off the hook. We'll see who laughs last."

I hang up the phone. I am not fazed. I have never had war openly declared on me before by a friend who is not a friend, but I have survived many battles right here under my own roof.

The man who is not my father is an enemy to be reckoned with. Billy Beezer does not frighten me at all. Kids from happy families should not declare war on kids who live in war zones.

I am now ready for my date. There is only one small problem, but, unfortunately, it is a serious small problem. I have scrounged up all the money that I possess in the world, including the nickels and dimes that I have been depositing in a jam jar for nearly a year, two five-dollar bills that I received for mowing lawns last summer, and several one-dollar bills that I have kept hidden from the world by using them as bookmarks in the most boring book in my collection, a history of cartography, whatever that means. My total net worth comes to nearly eighteen dollars.

But what happens if my date with Gloria calls for an expenditure of twenty dollars? Or even twenty-five dollars? I have never been on a date with a girl like Gloria before. To be frank, I have never been on a date with any kind of girl before. So I do not know exactly what to expect. But it strikes me that a girl who lives on Beechwood Lane, up near the golf course, and who owns half of a horse, is used to being treated a certain way.

She did suggest that we should eat dinner together at the Center Street Diner, after the game. Gloria clearly has a healthy appetite, judging by the way she gulped down my date proposal note. Perhaps she skipped lunch today, to be in top eating form. Perhaps, slender as she is, she will want a salad before her hamburger. She may even be in the habit of finishing off her dinner dates with a nice slice of apple pie.

The conclusion is inescapable. I need reserve funds. This is not the first time this had occurred to me. I was planning to borrow some money from my mother, but she is still not home from the factory.

I glance at my watch. If I am to pick up Gloria on

time, so that we can get good seats at the basketball game, I should go now. I cannot wait for my mother.

This leaves me with two alternatives. Neither of them is a particularly pleasant option.

Among the Lashasa Palulu, when the tribe is threatened by a dire event, as, for example, an invasion of fire ants, an emergency council is called. The difficult options are debated. Should they abandon their village to their insect foes? Should they put on enormous shoes and attempt to stomp out the tiny six-legged invaders? Should they sacrifice to the gods, throw a big, drunken party, and trust that everything will work out for the best?

Once all the options have been put forth and debated, they take a vote, and choose a course of action. After that vote, it is forbidden on penalty of death ever to mention again any of the alternatives that were considered but not chosen.

The salient point here, whatever that means, is decisiveness at a time of crisis.

Here are my two options. I can go on the date with Gloria knowing the whole time that I may run out of money and be disgraced. Or I can borrow some money, just in case it is needed, and return it later.

The only other money in the house belongs to the man who is not my father. He keeps it in a secret stash, a hiding place that he believes I do not know about.

My body is primed for my big date. Adrenaline is coursing through my veins. In my gray corduroy pants, I feel worldly and masterful. I am afraid of nothing.

I walk down the hall. I enter the bedroom shared by my mother and the man who is not my father. I walk directly to his bureau. Open the upper sock drawer. Carefully I move at least two dozen pairs of socks to one side. I do not have time to consider the question why a man who has only two feet needs so many pairs of socks.

At the bottom of the sock drawer is a knitted bootie. It is heavy—crunchy to the touch. I open it . . . and see more money than I have ever seen before. The man who is not my father has an impressive stash. Clearly, he does not believe in banks. Or maybe he is planning to start his own bank. There are many twenties. There are fifties. I even glimpse several crisp hundred-dollar bills.

I take only one twenty. I start to replace the

bootie . . . and then I feel something beneath it. Something small and hard that clearly does not belong in a sock drawer.

It is wrapped in a blue towel. I know I have no business looking at it, but there is a very good reason why I am curious. Whatever it is, it must be even more valuable than money, since the man who is not my father has buried it at the very bottom of his sock drawer, beneath his secret money stash.

I need to find out what is more valuable than money.

I carefully lift the blue towel out of the drawer. It is unexpectedly heavy. I unwrap it. Metal glints. I feel myself shiver.

It is a gun. To be accurate, it is a pistol.

12

the Bonanza Ranch House

Who is this young man who strides so purposefully along Beechwood Lane, checking his watch every time he passes under a streetlight? I do not recognize him. He is dressed in gray corduroy pants and a green sweater—my pants and my best Christmas sweater—and with his hands tucked into the pockets of his tan jacket he is doing a very good impersonation of me.

But he cannot be me. Because I would never have the nerve to cross Highland Avenue and head the final block along Beechwood Lane toward Gloria's house. And there the one-story house is, less than a hundred yards away, all new and white and luxurious, spread out across a large lot of tall maple and cedar trees like the splendid ranch of a wealthy cattle herder.

This cannot be me, this handsome young man

who pauses, takes a deep breath, and forges bravely on toward the house. He looks like me. He walks like me. He is even whistling a stupid little song that I know. But he cannot be me. I would never have such nerve.

It is bad enough that nobody knows who I am. Now I don't even know who I am. Someone who looks like me, but is dressed better than me, and is braver than I am, although an equally bad whistler, is trying to steal my big date.

The young man who is not me stops in front of the Great Bonanza Ranch House. It is, of course, not a real ranch house, and it has nothing to do with any bonanza, but for the purposes of this optimistic chapter I will call it the Great Bonanza Ranch House, for three reasons. It is easily the largest house I have ever been this close to entering. It is so spread out, and occupies so much land, that it looks like a ranch house to my untrained eye. And dwelling inside its comfortable walls is the greatest bonanza I can imagine—this is the house where Glory Hallelujah rises every morning, dew-fresh from her satiny bed linen, to shower and dress for school.

The young man who is not me lingers in the shadows for a moment. Has he heard something? Perhaps he has the strong feeling that someone is following him, and watching his every step.

A unique and eerie bird trill suddenly breaks the small-town silence. It sounds like the battle honk of a wild Javan parrot. But since there are no wild Javan parrots in my town that is not a town, the young man who is not me looks around nervously.

Is there a Beezer afoot? If Billy Beezer is indeed behind the ominous birdcall, he is well hidden. The night holds only deep shadows.

The young man who is not me moves forward. Trips on a curb. Flails his arms around wildly. Falls to the neatly manicured lawn. Gets up quickly. Checks to see if there are grass stains on the knees of his gray corduroy pants. Glances up at the house to see if anyone has witnessed this act of colossal awkward-ness.

Ah, so it is me after all.

I recover my balance. Head up the front walk.

On the door is a lion's-head knocker. To one side is a lighted doorbell button. Do I ring or do I knock?

Faced with this difficult question, I take several last seconds. I check my fly. It is zipped to the top floor, so to speak. I put my palm up in front of my face and smell my breath. It is not exactly lemony fresh, but it also will not wilt rose bushes at ten paces.

Another odd birdcall sounds behind me, so loudly that it nearly knocks me off the porch. This time it is no wild Javan parrot. I believe what I have just heard is the blood-hungry death hoot of the Giant North American Sheep-Eating Gray Owl. This ferocious member of the owl family has been thought by bird experts to be extinct for more than a century, but apparently there is at least one surviving specimen, and he sounds like he is within fifteen feet of me, and hovering.

Clearly there is no more time to waste.

I ring the doorbell.

Footsteps approach. The big wooden door is opened inward and I find myself looking at a very beautiful blond woman in a blue dress, who is smiling at me with sparkling white teeth. No, this is not a movie star. This, I realize, is Mrs. Hallelujah, Glory Hallelujah's mother, and one day Gloria will look like this, and that is not such a bad thing.

I have never been smiled at by anyone this elegant before. My nose has never encountered anything like the expensive perfume she is wearing. I do not know what to do, so I, in fact, do nothing. I do not move a muscle. I do not identify myself. I do not blink or tremble or even open my mouth to breathe. I just look back at her like an idiot.

"You must be John," she says. "I'm Mary Kay Porter." She extends her right hand and enfolds my own in it, for a heartbeat. It is not a firm handshake. Her hand is not really a hand at all. It is really a puff of cloud—a warm, soft bit of sun-warmed vaporous sky. "Please come in," she says.

I follow Mrs. Hallelujah into the Great Bonanza Ranch House and the big wooden door closes behind us. We are now protected from whatever North American Sheep-Eating Gray Owls happen to be hovering in the vicinity. We are in a zone of luxurious peace and security.

Heavenly music is being pumped in, seemingly from all directions. The plush carpet beneath my feet is several inches thick, so that I sink into it with each step, as into cottony quicksand. Even the air is redolent, whatever that means, with a sugary aroma of fresh-baked dainties that wafts in from the kitchen and makes my mouth water.

I find that I have stopped walking. I am standing in the hallway of the Great Bonanza Ranch House, momentarily paralyzed by pleasurable sensory overload. My central nervous system congratulates my brain, and at the same time delivers a stern warning: "Listen up, dunderhead. You have finally blundered into paradise. Pitch your tent here. Begin a new life. Do not go back to that house that is not a house and that life that is not a life or I warn you, I will remain here, and all your nerve fibers, synapses, and sensory organs from your nose to your toes will do likewise."

My brain has never before been threatened with a revolt by its own central nervous system. It freezes and locks. I am aware that I am standing there, stock still, inhaling the sugary smell and listening to the choir of angels, and the only sign of life that I am giving off is an occasional blink.

Mrs. Hallelujah also stops walking, and studies me. "John? Are you all right?"

"Yes," I manage to whisper. "This music . . . It's very beautiful."

She smiles. "Some people find the harmonies and dissonances a little unusual. But I like the adventure of musical impressionism. Don't you?"

136

Mrs. Hallelujah, I wouldn't know musical impressionism if it flew down from the chandelier and spat in my eye.

"Yes," I say.

"Do you listen to much Debussy at home?"

Mrs. Hallelujah, not to be gross, but at my home the closest we get to unusual harmonies and dissonances is when my dog barks and the toilet flushes at the same time. "Of course. When we have the time."

"Yes. You must make time for the beautiful things in life." Mrs. Hallelujah closes her eyes, tilts back her head, and for several seconds lets the music wash over her like summer rain. She looks sad, and very beautiful. In a soft voice she tells me, "This is his 'Prelude to the Afternoon of a Faun.' It was inspired by a poem of Mallarmé."

Mrs. Hallelujah, you are a wonderful woman. I suspect that you know all there is to know about music and about French poets. Furthermore, Mallarmé, whoever he was, may have written about fauns, but you went him one better—you raised a fawn. There is very little that I can say to a woman such as yourself except congratulations, well done, and please don't hold it against me if I lie to you throughout this entire conversation. You see, if I told you the truth—that I know absolutely nothing about music, or art, or poetry, and that, in fact, the music police have a long-standing warrant out for my arrest—you might not let me take your precious fawn to the basketball game.

We begin walking again. The hallway seems to go on forever. Paintings hang on the walls in wooden frames.

"Gloria tells me you are quite musical yourself," Mrs. Hallelujah says. "You're in the band, aren't you? What do you play?"

I begin to answer, and the two-syllable word catches on my tongue. It is the first time I have ever realized that I play an unglamorous instrument. I wish I could tell her "I strum the harp." Or "I tinkle the piano keys now and then." Instead, I hear myself saying, "I play the tuba."

"The tuba?" she repeats. "How . . . courageous of you. All that brass and piping. I'll never know how people get a sound out of it." Somehow she makes me feel like I am the plumber of the music world. Then she smiles at me. "Gloria should be down in a moment. Why don't you go into the study and say hello to Gloria's father."

She ushers me toward a doorway and calls out, "Fredrick, come meet John. He's here to take Gloria to the basketball game." She gives me a little push through the doorway, and whispers, "I'm making some ginger snaps and they should be just about ready. I'll bring them in a minute."

I am propelled into the study by the gentle push from Mrs. Hallelujah. The study has bookshelves filled with books. Some of the books have leather bindings, and the room has a smell of old wood and leather. A wood fire burns cheerfully in the fireplace.

A solidly built man with broad shoulders and strong, handsome features stands up from a desk as I enter the room. He has a great chin and a most impressive forehead. They look to me like they belong on Mount Rushmore, carved between the faces of Theodore Roosevelt and Abraham Lincoln. "Well," he says, moving around the desk toward me with surprising speed, "so you're the young man I've been hearing so much about."

My hand is seized in a strong, warm vise of a grip. My fingers are pressed together as if the intent is to wring orange juice out of them. My right arm is pumped so hard I believe it actually rips free from my body, but it manages to cling to its socket by two or three tenacious tendons. "How are you doing? It's John, right? How are you doing, John?"

"Fine, sir." I believe you have just rearranged my skeletal system, but it's still a pleasure to meet you.

"You don't have to call me sir. Mr. Porter will do. Or heck, even Fred. Why don't you come have a seat by the fire here, and we'll get a good look at each other. My little ducky—I mean, my Gloria—tells me you're a math whiz."

Sir. Mr. Porter. Fred—I will follow you over to the fireplace and I will sit down across from you on this oxblood leather armchair, and I will attempt to avoid catching on fire myself, but let me assure you right now, I am not a math whiz. I am not even a Cheez Whiz. I am no kind of whiz. "No, sir. Math is real hard for me."

"Modest, eh? I like that. But my Gloria tells me you correct the teacher. She also tells me you're an athlete. Soccer, right?"

I am not nodding, Mr. Porter. That would be confirming a lie. I am merely moving my head front to back because it feels like I am starting to singe my hair.

"I don't know much about soccer, to tell you the

truth. My game was football. I was a running back. You know what my nickname was, John?"

"No, sir."

"Bulldozer. You know why they gave me that nick-name?"

"No, sir."

"I used to run people over. Squash them. Obliterate them, really. Well, it was just part of the game."

You do not have to defend yourself to me, sir. I am not blaming you. No doubt you had every right in the world to pave football fields with the flattened corpses of your opponents.

"John, enough about football. Let's talk about something more serious for a moment. Do you run track?"

"No, sir."

"Neither did I, John. But here's my point." Why are you suddenly leaning forward, sir? I can hear you just fine. Why are you now putting your rather large hand on my rather small shoulder? "It's not a race, John. Get me?"

I am trying to follow you, Mr. Bulldozer, sir, with every gray brain cell at my feeble command, but you have lost me. "Uh . . . not quite. What's not a race?"

Why are you lowering your voice almost to a whisper? Is your chin quivering—is it preparing to bludgeon me, or could that just be my imagination?

"I'm a straight shooter, John. I know you and Gloria are young and full of beans. Heck, I'm not that old myself. I remember how it is. The old Bulldozer had a pretty hot engine in his day. But, you know, it's not a race, John."

"No, sir. I mean, yes, sir, it's not, sir." I still have no idea on earth what you are talking about, but I am positive that you are one hundred percent correct.

"There's plenty of time, John. Plenty of turns in the track."

"Yes, sir."

"Because I'll be honest with you, if I thought somebody tried to take advantage of my little ducky . . . well, I'd . . . I'd . . ." Mr. Porter, your face no longer looks like it belongs on Mount Rushmore—it now looks like it belongs in the FBI's file bank on men most likely to commit crimes against humanity. And the grip of your hand on my shoulder has become so tight that I believe your fingerprints will remain on my skin for the rest of my life.

"Dad?" Glory Hallelujah has materialized in the doorway. She is wearing very tight black pants and a silky blue top that accentuate the curves of her young and highly nubile body. If I were not in the presence of her father, the human bulldozer, and if he did not have me in his Vulcan death grip, I would describe it as an extremely sexy outfit. As it is, let me just say that my date for the evening looks quite lovely.

"Ah . . . my little ducky." The smile snaps back to Mr. Hallelujah's face and he releases me from his grip of death.

"I told you not to call me that," Gloria says.

"She's so cute, isn't she?" Mr. Hallelujah says to me, with a wink. "John and I were just getting acquainted."

I step a bit away from Mr. Hallelujah, and glance at my watch. "Maybe we should be going. We don't want to miss the tip-off."

Glory Hallelujah walks over to me, slips her fingers into my own, throws a look at her father that I can't even begin to interpret—and then she surprises me by stepping even closer and kissing me on the cheek. "John," she says, "you look nice. Umm, you smell nice."

Mr. Hallelujah's face begins to turn an unusual shade of red. It is the color a volcano turns when it is trying to not erupt by swallowing down large quantities of molten lava. "John," he rumbles, "remember what we talked about . . ."

I would like to talk to you further, Mr. Hallelujah, but as you can see, I am being pulled toward the door by your little ducky of a daughter, whose feather-soft fingers are far more pleasant than your death grip, so *hasta la vista* . . .

But Mr. Hallelujah does not give up. He is following after us, muttering phrases. "About track . . . about things that are not a race . . . You don't want to make a mistake early on that could cripple you . . ."

Mrs. Hallelujah has materialized on the other side of us. "Ginger snaps, hot and crusty!" she sings out, and pops some small and delicious tidbit in my mouth.

With the sugary dainty melting on my tongue and Mr. Hallelujah's veiled warnings ringing in my ears, Gloria and I leave the Great Bonanza Ranch House and set off toward our anti-school through the autumn darkness.

13

my big date

"Thanks for putting up with my parents," Gloria says as we walk down Elm Street hand in hand.

"They're really nice," I say.

"Be glad you don't have to live with them," she responds. "They're completely nutso."

Gloria, I fear you lack knowledge about the true range of the parental nutso scale. If you would like to come over to my house that is not a house and spend a few hours with the man who is not my father, you might reappraise, whatever that means, your opinions about your mom and dad. "Your house is also real nice," I tell her.

"It's okay," she says. "Mindy Fairchild's house is much bigger."

Just then, a ferocious growl explodes near us like a howitzer blast and reverberates down the block. Glory Hallelujah ducks her head instinctively, and grabs my hand tighter. "Good lord, what was that?"

I hesitate to tell her that, to me, it sounded very much like the frustrated roar of a Siberian bull walrus who has been scorned during mating season by all the cows and has spent the last several days grinding his tusks against the ice in solitary fury. I do not offer this opinion to Gloria. I also decide not to tell her that it may be Billy Beezer, my friend who is not a friend, tracking us through the darkness. I do not want to alarm her with the thought that we are being stalked by a convicted egg roll felon. "Maybe it was a hungry squirrel," I suggest.

"Squirrels don't roar," she says, and as an amateur naturalist myself, I find it hard to argue with this observation. She peers nervously into the darkness. "C'mon, what do you think it was, really?"

Among the Lashasa Palulu, when it becomes necessary to inform the female members of the tribe of an unpleasant situation—such as, for example, an impending attack by giant and invincible cannibal warriors—it is their practice to break the bad news in small and non-threatening installments. "We're going to have some company soon, dear," a Lashasa warrior might say to his wife. "Some very hungry company. In fact, there may soon be a feast the likes of which neither of us will probably ever see again."

I decide to adopt this line of response with Gloria. "You know, one of the great things about having friends is that you're never quite sure when or where they're going to pop up," I say.

"Like that has something to do with anything?" she mutters, scanning the darkness for signs of large predators.

"Just that we'll probably end up meeting some of my friends at the game tonight," I continue. "As I'm sure we will meet some friends of yours."

"Mindy Fairchild may be there," Gloria says, "but if she expects us to sit with her, she can just forget it."

"It is even possible that we may meet some friends on the way to the game," I say gently, giving her hand a comforting squeeze. "Friends who are having problems that might make them act a little weird." Gloria stares at me—she may be deciding that I am as nutso as her parents. "Gloria, have you ever been in a situation where one of your friends from school—or even somebody who's not a real close friend—is a little jealous of you?" I ask.

She relaxes—I have apparently hit a topic she

likes to talk about. "Oh, sure, isn't that just the worst," she says as if it happens to her every hour of every day. "Kim Smallwood is so jealous of my hair that she tries to copy it right down to the highlights and the bounce. But I can't help it if my hair is naturally blond and full-bodied and hers is like fishing line. And Julie Moskowitz saw my Anna Sui mini and bought one just like it for herself, but with her knees she should concentrate on covering up rather than showing off. And Yuki Kaguchi stole my shade of lipstick, and said that she was wearing it first, but everyone knows she's a little liar."

I am trying to follow this list of small crimes and misdemeanors perpetrated against my beloved by her jealous friends, but I admit my head is reeling.

"But the worst of all," Gloria continues, now rolling with a full head of steam, "is when Mindy Fairchild goes around saying that I'm jealous just because her father earns more than my dad and they live in a bigger house on more land and Mr. Fairchild drives a new Lexus Coupe with calfskin seats and a Steadson-Olson speaker system. Can you imagine her saying that? As if I would care?"

"Why should you?" I agree. "Money isn't really that important."

"Absolutely. Her father doesn't earn that much more than mine," Gloria says. "She's just jealous of me because Luke loves me more than he does her, and when we both walk into the stable he comes to me first and nuzzles me, even if she puts an apple in her pocket to cheat, which she always does, but it doesn't help, because animals know what people are really like."

Glory Hallelujah is in a righteous rage. I keep silent and feel her soft hand in mine and think how lucky I am to be walking with her. "And the truth is," she tells me, "I don't think her house is really that special—it may be big and expensive but it's such an ugly puke color and there are rats in the cellar—real rats, the size of little dogs! I swear, I'm glad I don't live there. And I don't care at all for her family's new Lexus, although she could offer me some more rides in it if she wasn't such a sulky sourpuss, always upset 'cause Luke won't even wiggle his ears for her. And I think she has bad breath, too, only don't you dare tell her I said so."

We are now very close to our school that is not a school. There are cars pulling into the two parking lots and dozens of students streaming toward the main doorway. I am prepared to make my grand entrance with my big date. This is an important moment in my up-till-now-miserable life that is not a life. Glory Hallelujah will be, of course, the belle of the ball—or rather ball game—in her tight black jeans and silken blue top. I do not mean to be critical of my other charming female school mates who have no doubt labored hard to make themselves appear attractive on this autumn night, but they all look like a herd of yaks compared to the fawn I am escorting.

The foolish and highly judgmental taste arbiters of my anti-school are about to realize that they have been ignoring a very special person. No doubt they will all line up during halftime and apologize to me for their past rudeness and shortsightedness. As we approach the main entrance I am trying to decide if I will forgive them.

Glory Hallelujah lets go of my hand. "I guess we don't need the PDA stuff," she says.

"PDA?" I repeat, my hand now grasping only empty air.

"Public display of affection. I mean, we don't want people to think we're—you know, going out, and, you know, a couple, just 'cause we're going to a stupid basketball game together. Right?"

"Right," I say.

"People are so stupid. They think things that are not real are real, but they gossip about them as if they are real, and in a weird way they can kind of make them real, even though they're not real. Do you know what I mean?"

I look at my date who is apparently not a date and nod, even though I do not comprehend so much as a word of the complete drivel she is spouting, beyond the fact that she has constructed some type of elegant intellectual rationale, whatever that means, for ruining my grand entrance. "Absolutely," I say. "I've often thought the same thing, but I've never put it into words."

And then we are swept up in the human tide of students and families and carried along through hallways and down stairways toward our old anti-school gymnasium. Several times during this procession I am poked from behind with enough force to make me stumble. Each time this happens I believe I hear faint, mocking laughter—the exact type of laughter, in fact, that one might expect from a jealous lunatic.

But when I whirl around expecting to confront a familiar face with a prominent beezer, I spot no one I can single out and blame for shoving me. Either Billy Beezer has gotten much better at quick getaways since his apprehension by the Wong Chong chef, or I am suffering from the paranoid delusions that quite understandably may accompany going on a date that is not a date to a school that is not a school to watch a basketball game that will not be a basketball game.

It will not be a basketball game because on this night our team, the Friendly Beavers, is matched up against the best team in the county, the Saber-Toothed Tigers of Fremont Valley.

We reach our old anti-school gymnasium. A big American flag hangs down from the high steel girders at half-court. The wooden bleachers are already filling up with Beaver hopefuls and Saber-Toothed Tiger loyalists. "Remember, we are not under any circumstances going to sit with Mindy Fairchild," Gloria says, scanning the crowd.

We pass several people I know. Violent Hayes walks by us, heading in the other direction. Her gaze flicks from me to Gloria to me again. For a moment, our eyes meet. Why are you looking at me that way,

Violent Hayes? She does not answer, but she must be distracted by something, because she swerves suddenly and bangs into Gloria, nearly knocking my lovely date off her feet in a maneuver very similar to a hockey check. "Excuse me," Violent Hayes says.

"Clod," Gloria mutters as we walk on.

We pass Mrs. Moonface, who is wearing an old high school jacket that I believe dates back to her days as a student in our anti-school. She is sitting by herself. In the algebra room Mrs. Moonface inspires terror, but sitting all alone on a bleacher she appears rather pitiful. As we pass her, I send her a telepathic poem that I make up on the spot:

> *Mrs. Moonface, as you can see,*
> *I, who know nothing of geometry,*
> *And less of algebra, am here with my cute date,*
> *While you, Mrs. Moonface, who can equate,*
>
> *And divide and factor like a computer,*
> *Are all alone, the loneliest Beaver rooter.*
> *When it comes to increasing one's happiness*
> *All the math in the world is clearly powerless.*

Mrs. Moonface does not respond to my poem, because all her energy is being directed toward trying not to look sad and lonely. She has a magazine on her lap and a camera around her neck, and she keeps glancing toward the doorways, as if at any second she expects a handsome man named Jacques to appear bearing a sandwich tray and escorting Clark Gable, her date for the evening.

Mrs. Moonface, I do not mean to be cruel, but there are no handsome men named Jacques in the vicinity, and the only sandwiches served during our basketball games are hot dogs and tuna melts sold by the Veterans' Wives Auxiliary. And the chances of Clark Gable appearing tonight as your date would be far in the negative range, even if he were not dead, which I am quite certain he is.

Meanwhile, Glory Hallelujah is leading me along at a rapid clip, her eyes raking eagerly over the hundreds of people settling in on the rows of bleachers. "They must be sitting right smack in the middle of the Beaver cheering section. Mindy's so predictable. Oh my God, there's Yuki Kaguchi! And look, she dared to wear my personal shade of eyeliner, the little thief. And there's Julie Moskowitz—I see she's got her bony little sparrow legs all covered up for once. Wise move."

A note of panic begins to sound in Gloria's otherwise musical voice as she continues to scan the gymnasium. "But I don't see Mindy Fairchild. She's probably home doing her English homework with Toby Walsh. Which is fine by me, because I think Toby's almost as much of a loser as she is, and even if they were here, we absolutely would not sit anywhere near them."

That is good news for me, because Toby Walsh is the handsome star of the football team, and I have no desire to sit near him, where the ten million kilowatts of his social-status star power will completely eclipse the few feeble volts of juice that I occasionally give off.

The two teams run out and begin warming up. The audience roars as the Friendly Beavers go through a lackluster layup drill while the Saber-Toothed Tigers dunk ball after ball with such fury that the rim seems in danger of snapping. I believe the time has come for us to sit down, but Gloria is not slackening her pace in the least.

We pass Mr. Steenwilly, who is sitting ten bleachers

up, with his arm around a pleasant-looking woman with long red hair and striking green eyes. She must be Mrs. Steenwilly. He sees Gloria and me pass by, smiles broadly, waves, and points us out to Mrs. Steenwilly.

I know exactly what you are thinking, Mr. Steenwilly. You believe that we are kindred spirits. You feel you understand me, and that just as you have apparently persuaded some lovely lady that Arthur Flemingham Steenwilly is a keeper, I have now done the same with Glory Hallelujah. You feel that I am therefore a successful chip off the old Steenwilly, and that thought evidently gives you pleasure.

But the truth, Mr. Steenwilly, is that you don't know me from Adam, whoever he is. You don't know me at all. And the only thing I will tell you about myself, Mr. Steenwilly, is that we really have absolutely nothing in common. You are a talented man, cut out for great things, who is temporarily on a doomed crusade to bring light to our anti-school.

And I am a shipwreck survivor, clinging to a raft that is slowly disintegrating while hungry sharks swim in circles beneath me and starfish ring dinner bells with each of their five arms. So why don't you turn back to Mrs. Steenwilly and peer into her striking green eyes and stop waving and staring at me with that big, goofy smile running parallel to the thin mustache on your face.

Gloria's head suddenly stops rotating. *"There they are, right next to the Tigers' section!"* Gloria says. "Of course they think they're too cool to sit with everyone from their own school. They're so predictable. Come on."

"I thought we weren't going to sit near them," I say, attempting to keep pace with her. I am beginning to suspect that Gloria may in fact be a goat and not a girl after all, because her climbing ability as she springs from bleacher to bleacher seems more caprine than human, whatever that means.

We reach the bleacher where Mindy Fairchild and Toby Walsh are seated. Mindy is a very pretty dark-haired girl who I don't know very well since we have no classes together and on the social-status ladder of our anti-school she is at the very top while I am under the rock that props up the lowest rung. Not merely is

her date for the evening, Toby Walsh, the best athlete at our school, but his broad shoulders, which
resemble the shoulders of a Brahma bull, his tropical
rain forest of curly brown hair, and his good-natured
aw-shucks grin make him a likely candidate for future
matinee idol and multiple Oscar winner, if he is not
too busy leading the NFL in rushing.

Gloria stops when we reach their bleacher. She
puts her hands on her hips rather dramatically. "So,
I was beginning to think you two weren't coming,"
she says to Mindy as if a dirty trick has been played
on her.

"What are you talking about?" Mindy replies
coolly. "We've been here for twenty minutes. You're
the one who's late."

This makes so much sense that Gloria switches
tack. "Well, I was kind of busy with Luke," she says.
"Some of us have obligations. Some of us were giving
care and affection to animals that need us and love us
and depend on us."

"What makes you think I haven't been doing a little
of that tonight?" Mindy asks with a smile, and nestles
her head against Toby's mountainside of a shoulder.
As if responding to a secret order, he puts his arm

around her. They are, in fact, a very attractive couple.

Suddenly I feel Gloria's hand slip into my own. And I believe one entire side of her body is suddenly and inexplicably pressing up against me. The Supreme Court must have repealed the rule against PDAs without notifying me.

Gloria sits down next to Mindy on the bleacher, dragging me down alongside her. For someone who has mentioned several times that she does not intend to sit next to Mindy, she has by some accident of fate ended up very close to her indeed. In fact, she is practically sitting on Mindy, and she is also quite close to Toby, who she smiles at periodically in what is doubtless a friendly and innocent fashion.

"You may have forgotten," Gloria says to Mindy, "but Friday is Owner Care Day. But don't worry, Luke and I had an extra-special wonderful time this afternoon. You know, he gets so lonely when I'm not there. I brushed him till he made that happy sound in his throat. And I fed him a little snack. He ate it right out of my hand."

Mindy rolls her eyes, and shrugs her shoulders very slightly, as if to say, "Oh, no, don't bring up that Luke nonsense again."

Toby appears confused. He looks at me. "Are you Luke?"

"No," I say, "I am John. Luke is a horse." I consider adding that Gloria does not brush me, and that I do not eat snacks out of her hand, but I have to admit I would not completely rule out either of those if the chance arose later this evening.

"Luke is *our* horse," Mindy tells her broad-shouldered date. "Gloria and I each own half of him."

"Yes, and we're supposed to share taking care of him," Gloria says. "I guess some people have more important things to do with their time. But don't worry, I fed him and brushed him down from the tips of his ears to the bottoms of his feet and now he's just fine."

Just then I hear a familiar voice behind me proclaim, with incontrovertible authority, whatever that means, "Horses don't have feet. They have hooves."

I turn and see Andy Pearce and Billy Beezer standing just below us on the bleachers.

"What do you know about horses' feet?" Gloria asks Andy. But what she is really asking is: "Who are you, you annoying little geek? And who is this strange-looking big-beaked bozo next to you? Is it really possible that we inhabit the same earth, or is this just a bad dream and when I wake up you will fade away into the nothingness you deserve?"

"I know that horses have hooves and not feet," Andy Pearce says. "Haven't you heard of hoof-and-mouth disease? They don't call it foot-and-mouth disease."

Gloria wisely decides not to argue this point, but she looks back at Andy as if she is fairly certain she can make him disappear by willing it and squinting her eyes a certain way.

Andy Pearce does not disappear. He turns to look at me. "John, how come you're not sitting with your friends?"

Billy Beezer steps forward. "Because we're not his friends, Andy. Not anymore."

"Whoever you are, why don't you sit down," Toby suggests. "The game's about to start."

"Allow me to introduce myself," Billy Beezer says, looking at Gloria with the same poorly disguised hunger he once focused on steaming Chinese appetizers. "My name is Bill Beanman. My parents named me William, but my friends call me Billy or just Bill. Except for one aunt who calls me Willy."

"If you don't quit blocking my view, I might have to rip your willy off," Toby growls.

Billy Beezer sits down very fast, but continues talking. He is now speaking directly to Gloria. "We actually sit near each other in math class. You may have noticed me."

Gloria does not deign to reply, but what she is thinking is: "If you were a cuticle and I had the right size scissors, I could snip you off and throw you away and be done with it."

"You may also have heard about my speech in the Student Council on behalf of adding a grapefruit juice option to our cafeteria selection," Billy Beezer says. "It was reprinted on the back page of *The Daily Beaver*."

I believe Billy Beezer is prepared to go on listing his Student Council achievements for some time, but at this moment a sonic boom rocks the gymnasium as the crowd roars for the opening tip-off. The Saber-Toothed Tiger center, who looks like a giraffe on stilts, barely has to leave his feet as he tips the ball to his point guard, who dribbles circles around our entire hapless Beaver squad and dunks the ball with enough force to crack the floorboards under our net.

"*Go, Tigers!*" a large and rather rotund young man sitting barely five rows in front of us shouts, and he holds up a large brass bell over his head and rings it furiously.

"Hey, tubby, pipe down and lose the bell," Toby suggests helpfully.

"Screw you. You're sitting in our section," the portly Tiger rooter replies.

"Yeah? Well, you're in our gym," Toby points out.

"Yeah? Well, your team sucks."

"Yeah, well, you're fat and your girlfriend's ugly."

"I'd like to hear you say that again."

"You're fat and your girlfriend's ugly. What are you going to do about it?"

"What are *you* going to do about it?"

Toby stands up. Walks down five rows of bleachers. The Tiger fan tries to stand also, but before he can hoist his considerable bulk to his feet, Toby grabs him by the shirtfront. With a clever twisting and shoving maneuver, Toby sends the large young man rolling down the bleachers like a one-man avalanche.

Unfortunately, the vanquished bell ringer was right about at least one thing. We are indeed in the Tiger cheering section. There are cries of "Did you see what he did to Chris? *Get him! Kill his friends, too!*"

I raise my hands. "Dear friends," I say with such authority that the gym quiets. "Let me remind you that we are met here, not on the field of combat, but for a sporting occasion. You have come to our school, in friendship, and we welcome you. Are not the Beaver and the Saber-Toothed Tiger both creatures of the same forest? And while I am speaking of the forest, allow me to mention that among the Lashasa Palulu, a tribe renowned for its manliness, when the animal-hide ball is being batted around with a rival tribe, it is considered not merely rude to lose one's temper but a sign of unworthiness."

Actually, I think of delivering this speech, but I do not get the chance because a full-scale riot is breaking out all around us, and I find myself trying to squeeze my way, on the subatomic level, inside the wooden framework of the bleachers. Unfortunately, I am unable to merge with the varnished wood. Right next to me, Mindy Fairchild is shrieking and kicking at the date of the dispatched Chris, who has apparently decided to avenge her boyfriend by pulling out Mindy's long black hair. Gloria is also yelling at full blast, in my direction, "SAVE ME, YOU IDIOT! DO SOMETHING!"

A dozen or so Tiger faithful charge up the bleachers, only to be met by Toby, who—with a remarkable impulse of self-sacrifice—flings himself at them, knocking them over like so many bowling pins. There are police whistles. Frantic announcements over the P.A. system are drowned out by the closer and more terrifying sounds of knuckles connecting with jaws and knees crunching noses.

Everyone is trying to climb over everyone else. Inspired by some self-preservation instinct perhaps inherited from an ancestral earthworm in my very distant evolutionary past, I drop to my knees, then to my stomach, and actually see light and space down there. I grab Gloria's hand. "This way. Crawl."

We slither on our stomachs beneath the churning mass of bodies, to the end of a bleacher, and slide down a metal support to the gym floor. We are still not out of the woods, so to speak, for—in a misguided attempt at crowd control—the police have completely sealed off the exits to our anti-school gym and are advancing in riot formation down every stairway.

Out of the corner of my eye I see a rather beefy policeman dragging Billy Beezer away by the scruff of his neck. It is, I believe, the very same policeman who arrested Billy at the Bay View Mall. "This time we're going to throw away the key," I hear him growl.

"I don't want to get arrested," Gloria wails. "Do something, you idiot!" Apparently, in her excitement, she has bestowed "idiot" on me as what is no doubt meant as an endearing nickname.

I lead her underneath the bleachers.

It is a dark space, latticed with dark metal pillars and wires, with hanging ropes and spiderwebs and faded streamers from proms of years gone by. Above us echo the thunderous sounds of the riot.

This is, in fact, not the first time that I have taken refuge beneath the bleachers. On occasion, to escape a particularly onerous and competitive gym class, I have slipped away beneath these very same bleachers. So I happen to know that there is a small and rarely used door in the back that leads to a supply room that leads to a janitor's closet that ultimately emerges into the boys' locker room.

Within two minutes, Gloria and I have made a successful escape, and we are walking away from our anti-school with the few lucky survivors of the battle royal in the gym.

It is an exciting feeling. Police cars and vans are speeding by, sirens shrieking. In one of those vans, no doubt, Billy Beezer is being whisked to some sort of maximum-security facility. Occasionally, the police cars themselves pull over to allow an ambulance unobstructed passage.

All of us streaming home on the sidewalks feel a common bond—we have survived a massacre and lived to tell the tale. Three blocks from our anti-school, Gloria and I are unexpectedly joined by Mindy Fairchild and Toby Walsh. He has blood on his face, and I believe somebody has torn off part of his ear.

"How did you guys ever get out of that gym?" Gloria asks them.

"The police were coming to arrest us, so Toby ran right through a wall," Mindy coos admiringly.

"Actually, it was a supply door and I just kind of gave it a good stiff shoulder," Toby says modestly. "How did you guys get out?"

Before I can explain that we crawled out on our stomachs like earthworms, I am surprised to hear

Gloria say, "John kicked out a window and we climbed out over the jagged shards of glass."

"Cool," Toby says, slapping me on the back. "Well done."

"It was one of those things that just had to be done," I mumble.

Mindy pairs off with Gloria and the two of them begin gossiping about who got arrested and who got their noses broken.

I find myself in the unlikely position of walking on ahead, with Toby Walsh, the most popular guy in our school. "So," he says, "you're going out with Gloria?"

"Yeah. I guess," I respond cautiously.

"She's pretty fine." He throws a backward look— our two dates are out of earshot. "So, you getting anything?"

I am not sure I understand his question, so I decide to answer without answering. "You know how it is."

"No, I don't know how it is," Toby says with a laugh. "I never went out with her. To tell you the truth, she wanted to go out with me, but I said no go."

"Why not?" I ask.

"Well, she's real cute, and I hear she's pretty wild, but she has the personality of a disease," Toby says. "And then there's her dad."

"I met him tonight," I say. "He seemed okay."

"Did you hear what he did to Jerry Dickman?"

"No," I say. "Who is Jerry Dickman?"

"Her last boyfriend. Her dad caught them in the basement together, and he nearly separated Jerry's head from his body."

We are suddenly rejoined by the two girls. "Okay, Toby," Mindy says, putting her arm around his waist, "time to take you home and get you patched up."

"Hell, this little scratch on the ear barely hurts," Toby says. "I've played with far worse injuries than this."

"Toby, for the millionth time, life isn't a football game," Mindy says, reeling him in a little tighter. "And would a little care and affection from little old me really be such a bad thing?"

Toby changes his mind very quickly. "Goodbye, you guys," he says to us. "This is where we turn off."

"Goodbye," Gloria says back to them. "I've got to take John home and get him patched up, too."

Suddenly we are alone, on the street, near Gloria's

house. "I actually don't believe I have anything wrong with me," I say to Gloria.

"I think I saw some bruises," she says. "We better give you a quick checkup. And anyway, my parents are almost definitely asleep by now. Come in, and we can get to know each other better."

I confess that I am torn, but at the same time, I confess that I do not want to end the night torn in half like Jerry Dickman. "I don't know if that's such a great idea . . ." I say.

But as I feebly protest, Gloria takes my right hand in her own, and I can feel myself being led toward the Great Bonanza Ranch House like a steer to the slaughter. And as we walk, Gloria whispers into my ear with her hot breath, "We'll go down to the basement. My parents never go down there at night. You don't have to worry about a thing. After all, what's the worst thing that could happen?"

14

the worst thing that could happen

I have some advice for you. If someone ever asks you what the worst thing that can happen is, don't do what you are about to do. Get out. Fake a heart attack. Escape while you can. Especially if you are an unlucky person anyway, and you've just been hexed by chapter 13.

The Great Bonanza Ranch House is quiet as we enter. There is no dissonant music. No ginger snaps are snapping. The bulldozer is apparently upstairs.

"This way," Gloria says, leading me to the back of the house. From the front, the Great Bonanza Ranch House looks like a one-story structure, but behind and to one side of the house the land falls away sharply, allowing a lower story.

We pass through a door and descend carpeted stairs to a large, dark, finished basement. The place smells of wood. Split logs are piled up near a brick fireplace. "My father splits those by hand," Gloria says, "can you imagine? What a waste of time. He does it with this big, mean ax he keeps as sharp as a razor. One stroke per log. Chop. Chop. Chop."

"I really, definitely think I should be going . . ." I say.

"Don't be in such a hurry, John," Gloria says, stepping closer to me. "We have lots of time."

I hear something behind me and spin around.

She laughs. "It's only D.D. My cat."

"What does 'D.D.' stand for?" I ask.

"Dead Dickman," she says. "It's kind of an inside joke. Why don't you take off your shoes, John."

"My shoes? Why?"

"Well, then we can snuggle up on the couch. I'll put on some nice music."

Now, it is an odd thing, but if you had asked me two weeks ago, or even a day ago, if I would like to kick off my shoes and snuggle up on a couch with Glory Hallelujah, my brain would have turned a cartwheel inside its cranial pan. But at this moment, when such a fantasy is about to become a reality, all that my brain can focus on is the necessity of immediate flight. "Get out," my brain is tapping out in desperate Morse code to the signal stations in near and remote provinces of my body. "Flee, fool. Or you will go down in history as the second Jerry Dickman, and one day there will be a cat in this basement named after you, too."

Unfortunately, my brain is no longer in control. Certain other parts of my body that good manners do not permit me to describe have seized the throne, so to speak, and are issuing orders in one- and two-word bursts: "Stay! Sit! Unshoe yourself!" I find myself, therefore, sitting on the giant couch, taking off my shoes.

Suddenly the single overhead light dims. Slow, pulsating music floods the basement. I do not believe that we are listening to Debussy. This does not sound like "The Afternoon of a Faun." This sounds like "The Evening by the Steamy Lagoon." Glory Hallelujah, I do not mean to question your choice of music, nor your sense of appropriate volume, but you have cranked this up so loud that I believe the entire basement is throbbing.

I myself have nothing against loud music, particularly if the girl who turned it on is now sashaying in my direction with a smile on her face and her two soft blue eyes glinting mischievously, like sapphires in twilight. But there is, as science has fully documented, a direct connection between loud sound stimuli and waking up suddenly in a bad temper. And the Great Bonanza Ranch House, while lovely and sprawling, is rather compact in vertical design structure. I am, of course, not an architect, nor am I an acoustics engineer, nor am I that familiar with the sleeping habits of bulldozers, but I am worried. I stand up and intercept Gloria several steps from the couch. "Maybe we should turn this music down. We don't want to disturb your parents."

"Don't worry about them," Glory Hallelujah reassures me. "My mother has already taken her sleeping pills, and my father sleeps with earplugs. Boy, it's hot in here. Don't you want to take off your jacket?"

Glory Hallelujah, I do not want to take off my jacket. I do not think that would be appropriate behavior, given the shortness of our close acquaintanceship.

"That's better. But you're wearing a sweater underneath. Why don't you take that off, too, Johnny?"

Here, Glory Hallelujah, I draw the line. This Christmas sweater was given to me by my dear old mother, and it would be ungrateful of me to remove it, not to mention inappropriate, given the fact that I am not wearing any undershirt beneath it . . .

"C'mon, silly, arms up."

Glory Hallelujah, are you even listening to me? Why do I have the feeling I am being shucked like an ear of corn? And please do not feel that I am getting too personal with this next question, but why is it that you are so intent on disrobing me when you have not removed a single thread or stitch of your own attire? Surely, if we are to snuggle up on the couch, we should be similarly costumed, or de-costumed.

"Now, let's see those soccer muscles," Glory Hallelujah says, lifting my Christmas sweater from my body and running her hands gently over my shoulders and down my back.

Of course, there are no soccer muscles anywhere on my body. There are not even Wiffle ball muscles. But Glory Hallelujah does not seem deterred.

"Mmmm, that's better. Now, why don't we lie down on the couch and get comfy."

I believe I hear something stirring upstairs. It sounds like a door slamming. Or maybe it's a footstep. "I think someone's awake upstairs," I gasp.

"That's just our house shifting in the wind. C'mon, relax. Don't you want to snuggle up with me?"

My brain begins making a chain of logical points based on an elemental meteorological observation, whatever that means: it is not a windy night. Therefore, the Great Bonanza Ranch House cannot possibly be shifting in the wind. Hence, the sound I have heard cannot have been produced by the shifting of the house, and must have been generated by someone within the house.

But, sadly, not only is my brain no longer in control, but it has been stripped of all governing powers and told to go sit in the corner. The other parts of my body that are now running the show are unimpressed by meteorological observations and chains of logic. They do not care a whit for sounds in the night. They are focused on the vision of loveliness who is smiling at me and leading me over to the couch, pulling me along by her hot little hand like a tugboat hauling an ocean liner toward an iceberg.

"Flee, flee!" my brain is saying. But I lie down on the couch, right on top of something. There is an angry meow, and D.D. the cat hops off, onto the floor. There is another, human meow and Gloria slips onto the couch next to me. "Now," she purrs, "give me one of those tuba-twanging kisses."

Gloria, let me set the record straight. My tuba is actually a giant frog pretending to be a tuba, and I treat it with the utmost respect. We do not kiss. We do not even shake hands. Furthermore, my tuba does not twang. It is not a word used to describe tuba music. Let me also confess at this late moment that I have never kissed a girl before, and I have no idea how to do it. Which may explain why I have just bitten your nose.

"Ow, you bit me."

"Did I? That wasn't a bite . . . it was a . . . love nip. Gloria, maybe I should leave now . . ."

"Here, turn your head. That's it. Wow, I heard that you were a good kisser."

Glory Hallelujah, I cannot imagine who you might have heard that from because until this moment no sentient life form upon this planet, whatever that means, from the eagle on high to the plankton floating in the dark ocean depths, has ever allowed my lips to approach within kissing distance. But while you are therefore almost certainly fibbing about my reputation as a good kisser, I do not mind at all. Lying here on this couch kissing you is the high point of my life. The music is nice—though loud; and the lighting is nice—though dim; and you feel very soft and warm and quite wonderful snuggled up next to me, and all would be good in the world if I did not suddenly hear a loud pounding.

Surely that is my heart. Surely that is the blood pounding through my arteries.

"GLORIA? GLORIA!"

Surely that is my innermost soul repeating your lovely name the way the autumn breeze memorializes the summer rose. But why does it sound like the voice of the Bulldozer?

"GLORIA, ARE YOU DOWN THERE? YOU'D BETTER BE ALONE!"

Gloria tenses noticeably. "Oh my God, it's my father. But don't worry—I locked the door."

"GLORIA, DON'T MAKE ME BREAK DOWN THIS DOOR."

I try to stand up, to flee, but Gloria is holding me on the couch. "There's no place to run, John. The garage door only opens by remote control, and I didn't bring the clicker down with us. But don't worry, my dad's full of hot air," she whispers to me.

"He'll never actually break down the door." And then she shouts up, "AS IF YOU COULD BREAK IT DOWN! AS IF YOU WOULD DARE!"

Gloria, in this alarming crisis, it is not in our best interest to provoke your dear father any further. A few gentle and conciliatory words to the older generation might be in order . . .

"WHY DON'T YOU JUST GO JUMP IN THE LAKE, YOU NITWIT!" she shouts up. "YOU DON'T SCARE ME FOR A SECOND!"

"GLORIA," the Bulldozer's voice thunders from on high. "YOU'D BETTER OPEN THIS DOOR RIGHT NOW, AND YOU'D BETTER BE ALONE, OR SO HELP ME, THERE'S GONNA BE A MASSACRE!"

"YOU FOOL! YOU PIG! YOU BIG, BRUTISH, BULLYING BUFFOON!" Gloria shouts back. "YOU CAN'T CONTROL ME. YOU HAVE NO POWER HERE. GO BACK TO BED AND LEAVE ME ALONE!"

KA-BAM! There is a crashing sound from atop the stairs. I believe the Bulldozer has just switched into a low gear and thrown his considerable bulk against the door, which has somehow held firm.

"HAH, I KNEW HE COULDN'T BREAK IT

DOWN!" Glory Hallelujah shouts up, seemingly a bit disappointed.

KA-BAM, *KA-BAM*. There is a tremendous double impact, and the sound of wood giving way before a human battering ram.

I suddenly find myself on my feet, looking up at the stairs.

"Oh my God," Glory Hallelujah says to me, sounding more than a little bit thrilled, "I think he did it. He really broke down the door!"

A hulking, vengeful figure appears at the top of the stairs. Now, as you will remember, Gloria turned down the basement light to create a romantic effect, so it is difficult to see all the way up the basement stairs with any clarity. But even in this dim lighting the muscular figure staggering down the stairs is unmistakably Gloria's father, the Bulldozer. Step by step, he lurches toward us with what I believe was once a doorframe wrapped around his massive shoulders like a gigantic wooden necklace. Halfway down the stairs, I believe, he spots me. Perhaps he even sees that I am shirtless. He stops and stares at me.

Now, Mr. Hallelujah, sir, Your Bulldozership, please do not think that anything untoward has been going on between me and your little ducky, for whom, let me add, I have the very highest respect. I have remembered your advice, that my basketball game date with your daughter is not a race, and I have done nothing racy. The mere ten-second snuggle that we exchanged can be viewed as an expression of scholarly friendship between two algebra-class desk neighbors. I would also like to point out that we are young and foolish, and that as you no doubt remember from your days as a youthful Bulldozer, occasionally the wheels loosen on their axles, if you know what I mean. But the hour is late, and we are all tired, so I will now be happy to leave if you will just let me by, sir.

I intend to say this to Gloria's father, but before I get the words out he reacts much the way the King of the Beasts does when he returns from a trot across the savanna to find that some foolish hyena has blundered into his lair and is imperiling one of his precious lion cubs. Gloria's father tilts back his leonine head and gives what can only be described as the type of bloodcurdling roar that shakes the entire forest down to the deepest roots of the tallest trees.

"Oh my God," Gloria says, "he's gonna kill you. And there's no way out. It's over. You're dead."

In the annals of the Lashasa Palulu, one moment stands out as an example of salvation from near extinction. On one unfortunate day, the entire tribe was surrounded and nearly wiped out in an attack by its most formidable enemies, the giant and invincible cannibal warriors. As the circle of hungry cannibals closed around them, the Lashasa chieftain jumped onto his hands and, clasping his feet together toward the heavens, prayed for darkness. Suddenly, wondrously, magnificently, the sun disappeared in a total eclipse. In the pitch darkness, the Lashasa tribesmen and women were able to scurry around and between and through the legs of the giant cannibals, and escape into the forest.

I would pray for another such eclipse, but unfortunately I am in an enclosed basement, lit by electricity. Meanwhile, the Bulldozer reaches the bottom of the stairs and heads in my direction, and the look on his enraged face gives me little doubt that he intends to rip the spine from my back vertebra by vertebra.

Adapting Lashasa Palulu tactics to my current predicament, I grab one of my shoes—which, at Gloria's urging, I took off and discarded before our ill-fated couch snuggle—jump onto the couch, and, using the couch as a springboard, leap toward the ceiling and take a wild swing at the single, already dimmed, lightbulb.

There is the sound of breaking glass, and suddenly the basement is plunged into complete and utter darkness. I land in that darkness, crashing down heavily onto something that I believe was once a coffee table, but which will never again hold coffee cups because I have smashed it to smithereens.

"DON'T THINK YOU CAN GET AWAY FROM ME IN THE DARKNESS, YOU LITTLE WEASEL," the Bulldozer roars. "I WAS TRAINED FOR JUNGLE NIGHT FIGHTING IN NAM."

This is not particularly good news, but I remind myself that we are not in Nam, and that even the Bulldozer cannot see in pitch darkness. I cower behind the couch, keeping perfectly still.

"Daddy, I'm afraid of the dark," Glory Hallelujah screeches. *Do something!*"

"I'm gonna do something all right," the Bulldozer reassures her. He sounds alarmingly close to me. "I'm gonna pulpify that boyfriend of yours." His footsteps thud only a few feet away. "I'm coming for you, lover boy," he says. "I hear your heart beating. I can smell your fear."

My entire body is now on red-alert emergency status, with my brain firmly back in control. Please do not allow any fear smells to escape, my brain commands my skin. Okay, my skin agrees. We are a team trying to survive here. All smell emission will be curtailed until further notice. The pores of my skin click shut. Heart, stop beating, my brain orders. Find another, quieter way to pump blood. My heart immediately suspends all pumping activity and improvises a new "slow trickle" system of blood irrigation.

There is a sudden loud pounce in the darkness, less than ten inches from me.

"There, now I have you by your little throat!" the Bulldozer declares with glee. "What do you have to say now, Romeo?"

The Bulldozer's jungle night fighting skills must have deteriorated a bit since Nam, because he in fact does not have me by the throat or any other part of my body. I am still crouched in the darkness, silent, without heartbeat, respiration, or odor emission. I believe he has, in fact, grabbed D.D. the cat, who squeals in terror and tries to escape from his grasp by biting his hand.

"AAAH, I'VE BEEN CAT-BIT!" the Bulldozer roars. "I'll turn that stinking feline into a scarf!"

"If you hurt my little D.D. I'll call the police," Gloria cries out with admirable but, in my humble opinion, slightly misplaced compassion.

A furry missile brushes by me as it hurtles toward a corner of the basement that I have not had a chance to explore. D.D. has evidently decided not to stick around and tempt fate.

I have always believed that in matters of survival humans have much to learn from their animal friends. If, for example, you are on a ship and you suddenly see rats leaping off into the water, I believe it is an early warning sign that the ship may be on fire and it is time to begin searching for a life raft. Now, it is true that a life raft will do me little good in my present predicament, but this basement is D.D.'s domain, so to speak, and it occurs to me that when faced with the prospect of being turned into an item of winter clothing, Gloria's cat will head for the nearest exit.

I follow in D.D.'s scurrying paw steps.

A new voice floats down from upstairs. I believe I hear the dulcet tones of Mrs. Hallelujah. She is no longer pondering Debussy and Mallarmé. In fact, she sounds alarmed. "What's going on down there?" she asks. "I called the police. They're on their way. They're sending two squad cars."

"Good work, honey," the Bulldozer shouts up to her. "Now get a flashlight."

"In a jiffy," she says. "There's one in the kitchen."

D.D. and I are now hiding in a far corner of the basement. He is trying to get around a carton that has been wedged against a wall. I move it for him. Without even a thank-you, he disappears through a tiny opening at the base of the wall. I bend down and feel the opening with my hands. It is what I believe is called a pet door—a small swinging door which allows small animals to enter and exit. Unfortunately, I am not a small animal.

"Here's the flashlight!" Mrs. Hallelujah sings out from the top of the stairs.

"Great, honey," the Bulldozer says, and I hear his footsteps climbing up to meet her.

A flashlight beam suddenly pierces the darkness.

The Bulldozer first sweeps it around in the vicinity of the couch. Then his search expands outward to the more distant corners of the basement.

I will be discovered any second.

I get down on my knees and then on my stomach, and attempt to wiggle out through the pet door. Sadly, my skull is wider than the little doorway, to say nothing of my shoulders and hips.

"*Where are you hiding?*" the Bulldozer shouts. "Dickman was lucky compared to what I'm going to do to you, you soccer stooge. I'll pulpify you. They'll have to pick you up with a sponge and carry you away in a pail. And then I'll pulpify that stinking feline."

I hear Gloria's concerned voice. "Mom! Dad's scaring my little D.D."

The flashlight beam is now swinging toward me along the dark wall. "Skull, make thyself smaller," my brain commands. "Shoulders, contract. Hips, narrow. Okay now, everyone, on three. One, two, three . . ."

It is amazing how true desperation aids the human endeavor. My body gives an all-out effort at transmogrification, whatever that means. Somehow I reduce myself to the size of a house cat for a matter of seconds as I wiggle out through the pet door. I bump my head. I scrape my knee. I believe some of the skin from my left elbow remains on one edge of the pet door. But the important thing is that somehow I get through it.

Sadly, I am not outside. I don't know where I am. I am crawling in complete darkness through some sort of narrow tunnel. There is a rank odor of cat. There are clumps of what I hope is, or was, fur. I am not enjoying my little crawl through the darkness, but I believe it would be less enjoyable to go back and face the Bulldozer. So I press on. Eventually I must reach the end of this cat crawl space.

Soon I do arrive at the end of the tunnel, but that is not a good thing. The tunnel ends in nothingness. I fall out into darkness, plummet four or five feet, and land heavily on a pile of branches that breaks my fall. I am outside the basement of the Great Bonanza Ranch House, at the lowest point on the property.

I do a quick inventory. I have minor cuts and bruises, but no bones seem to be broken. I hear a door opening near me. And the Bulldozer's angry growl.

"Flee," my brain commands. I stand and stagger away as quickly as I can. It is thrilling just to be alive.

When I am perhaps a hundred feet from the Great Bonanza Ranch House I hear police sirens. Then voices. High-powered searchlights begin sweeping the Bulldozer's property, but I am four backyards away—safely out of range.

It is only when I feel safe that I realize I am also very cold. In fact, I am freezing. That makes a certain amount of sense because my shoes, my Christmas sweater, and my tan jacket with all my cash zippered into one of its side pockets are still in Glory Hallelujah's basement.

I cannot go back to claim them.

Half-naked and shivering, I set sail for home sweet home.

15

a short haul

I do not know if you have ever had the experience of jogging home through the darkness on a cold night in late autumn, jacketless, shirtless, shoeless, and sockless, with cuts and bruises on your arms and legs, while two police cars cruise the darkness searching for you.

If you have not, perhaps you will fail to understand the necessity I feel to get within the walls of my house that is not a house as soon as possible. The night of my big date started out balmy, but the temperature has been dropping steadily. It has been a night of some exertion and much danger, and even a home that is not a home seems like a relatively pleasant place—a shelter in the storm, so to speak.

I begin the chapter this way to convince you that I have ample reason for not exercising proper caution in returning to a war zone. I do not conduct reconnaissance. I do not peer through all the windows on the ground floor. I do not crawl up the drainpipe like a cat burglar and pry open an upstairs window.

In fact, the front door is unlocked and I just walk on in.

My house is pitch-dark. I feel about for the light switch. Suddenly a hand grabs my right wrist in a grip that makes me cry out.

I smell the hot stench of whiskey breath. The voice of the man who is not my father hisses, "Where is it?"

"Where is what?" I ask, stalling for time, even though I believe I understand his question.

WHOP. The hard slap to the back of my head makes my vision blur and my ears ring. He holds me with his left and slaps me with his right. I cannot wriggle free. "Don't play games. Where's my money?" In the moonlight that streams in through a window, I can just make out his angry face.

"In my jacket pocket."

"And where's your jacket?" WHOP.

The second slap catches me on top of my ear and is so hard it would knock me off my feet if he weren't holding me tightly. There are tears in my eyes, and I am suddenly looking back at the man who is not my father through a kaleidoscope, so that his image keeps breaking apart and re-forming. "I had to leave it somewhere," I manage to gasp. And then, to prevent a third blow, I hastily add, "I can get it tomorrow."

My arm is twisted behind me in an agonizing grip that I believe professional wrestlers refer to as the chicken wing hold. "That's not good enough. I'll take it out of your hide, tonight."

"Let me go or I'll scream," I say, thinking that my mother must surely be home now.

"Make a sound and you'll regret it for weeks," the man who is not my father counters in a not very pleasant tone.

I expect to be marched on into the house for further interrogation and punishment, so I am surprised when the man who is not my father pushes me ahead of him, outside, into the cold darkness.

Now, it may seem strange to you that after escaping from a riot at my anti-school virtually unscratched, and then neatly extricating myself from a basement massacre, I cannot elude, outfox, or outfight the man who is not my father.

Allow me to share one simple and very frightening

truth with you: your real enemy is someone who knows you. And the better they know you, and the closer they are to you, the greater is their capacity to do you harm. Total strangers who get a little angry and lose control at sporting events are no real threat, if the proper caution is used. Protective fathers of pretty fourteen-year-old girls will shout and sputter, get loud and use strong language, but in the end they will retreat into their warm houses and leave you alone.

But the person who shares a part of your life, who lives with you and knows all your habits and has a keen insight into what you value most in all the world—this is the person to fear.

The man who is not my father frog-marches me to his truck and, holding me securely, unlocks the back. I guess what he is going to do and attempt to resist, but he jerks my arm up higher, so that I yelp in pain. I consider screaming at the top of my lungs for help, but I do not do it. Screaming for help at this point is an all-or-nothing gamble—the street is dark and empty, and I know that if I do scream and no one comes to help me, the punishment will be quick and merciless. I am not willing to take the chance.

He gets the door open and shoves me into the dark bed of the truck, hard, and I go sprawling onto the cold metal floor. By the time I get back to my feet, he has closed the door and I hear him fumbling with the lock on the outside.

I am caged. It is dark beyond dark. I can only tell which side of the truck is the back because I can still hear him there. I throw myself against the metal door, but it does not budge.

Then all is silent. I sit there wondering what he will do. Will he leave me here to starve? I hear a door opening and shutting near me. The man who is not my father has climbed into the cab of the truck. In a minute I hear a diesel engine turning over, sputtering to life. And then we begin to move.

It is cold. It is dark. And I am as scared as I have ever been in my life that is not a life. The truck travels a long way at a high speed. It is too dark for me to see my watch, so I do not know if we have been traveling for one hour or for three, but it feels like we could be in another town, or another state, or even another universe.

And then the truck slows to a crawl. I hear metallic

grating and rasping sounds. A heavy iron gate is being opened. The truck drives very slowly down an incline for another few seconds and comes to a complete stop.

For ten or fifteen minutes I am locked inside the four metal walls listening to activity all around me. I hear voices as people walk by the sides of the truck. Then I hear the padlock being taken off the back, and the door is opened.

"Get out," the man who is not my father says.

I climb down from the back of the truck. At first I think we are in a garage, because I spot the rusty hulks of several cars that have been stripped of different parts. With wheels off axles, doors missing, and seats ripped out, they look like patients deserted by their doctors in the middle of surgery. It also strikes me as possible that we may be in a basement because the truck traveled downward and we are in a big, gloomy space with no windows visible. The floor all around the truck is piled high with large cardboard cartons.

Besides the man who is not my father, I see three men in this large and gloomy space. Two of them are keeping to themselves, smoking cigarettes off in a corner. They are wearing dark pants and sweatshirts and do not even give me a curious glance.

The third man walks closer to the truck, and looks me over. He is short—just a little taller than I am. His scruffy white hair clings like a determined patch of winter weeds atop a small, cramped face; it looks as if his most prominent features—his nose, his mouth, and his eyes—are competing for space on the same undersized billboard. He studies me with a sour expression, and then asks the man who is not my father, "You sure?"

The man who is not my father replies, "You're the one who said we're a man short."

"I said a man."

"He'll work like a man. I'll make sure of that."

"I don't like it. He's a kid. He doesn't even have shoes."

"He doesn't need shoes."

"Come over here," the short man says to me.

"Leave him alone," the man who is not my father tells him.

It is very frightening to me that the man who is not my father is now my only protection. I have a strong intuitive feeling, whatever that means, that the men in this garage are not warm and loving people who nurture and respect adolescents as the leaders of tomorrow. The man who is not my father may well be the best of the lot.

The short man smiles very slightly. "I'll pay him half."

"You'll pay me what he's worth when we're done."

The short man looks inclined to argue. Then he simply says, "If he's worth anything," and walks off.

The man who is not my father looks at me. "Work hard and keep your mouth shut."

I nod.

"Say 'Yes sir.' "

I have never in my life called the man who is not my father sir, but I have also never in my life been this frightened before. We are looking right into each other's eyes. I hesitate a long beat and he sees my fear and my indecision. I can tell that he is enjoying this.

The little fellow who sits in the swivel chair at the control switchboard of my brain is a notorious coward. He pulls down on the big yellow "coward" lever. "Yes sir," I hear myself whisper.

"Louder."

"Yes sir."

The man who is not my father smiles. "Then get to work. It'll keep you warm."

I spend the next half hour helping the three men and the man who is not my father load the big cardboard cartons onto the truck. We work quickly and in silence, except for grunts and groans. For a while I have no idea what is in the cartons, except that they are all about the same size and they weigh an awful lot. Some of the cartons have loose flaps, and a few are pocked with jagged holes that appear to have been ripped into the side by sharp objects. While helping to lift one such carton, I peek through a hole and see enough to guess what's inside. We are lifting televisions. All together there must be more than one hundred brand-new wide-screen television sets.

I decide not to ask the man who is not my father, or his short business partner, if they have paid for these TV sets. Something tells me that they are what I believe is called in underworld lingo hot. I believe that the man who is not my father may be involved in fencing stolen goods. This would explain his occasional short hauls, and perhaps the wad of cash in his sock drawer. It might also explain his sole contribution to the furnishings in our house—the brand-new wide-screen TV that sits proudly on its oak throne in our dining room.

Of course, I have ample reason for hating the man who is not my father, and that may be coloring my judgment. It is possible that this is a legitimate business. But it occurs to me that few legitimate wide-screen TV outlets operate out of dark basements in the middle of the night.

We finish loading the boxes on the truck. "Get in the back," the man who is not my father commands me.

"Not a good idea," the short man says to him. "If those boxes shift, they'll crush him."

"Funny, I don't remember asking your advice," the man who is not my father says with his customary warmth and politeness. Then, to me, he says, "Inside. Now."

"Yes sir," I say, but what I am really saying is: "I do not want to climb back into this truck and be crushed by falling television sets, but, hateful as you are, I have designated you my commanding officer to get me through this night's battle, and I am prepared to temporarily bestow upon you a title of respect which you do not deserve, and to follow your orders." I climb into the truck, and find a little room between two rows of stacked cartons.

The sliding back door of the truck comes down, and once again I am in darkness, this time surrounded by a forest of TV sets. We travel for perhaps an hour. I hate to keep repeating the phrase "I have never been this frightened before in my entire life," but on this unfortunate night I keep setting new records in this particular Olympic category.

While I have always enjoyed the miracle of television, and have watched my share of stupid shows, I have no desire to die beneath a ton of TV sets. That, however, seems a distinct possibility, because each time the truck swerves or changes speed, I can feel the forest of TV sets shift around me. The big cartons are stacked three and four high, and if a stack should topple onto me, or one stack should fall into another stack, setting off a chain reaction, I would be reduced to a human pancake in less time than it takes to change channels.

You might think that the prospect of being squashed by home appliances is so terrifying that it would completely occupy my mind during this ride. But the little fellow in the swivel chair who runs the controls of my brain is such a competent coward that he is quite capable of handling two, or even three, horrifying thoughts at the same time. And there is another thought—an insight, if you will—that keeps pestering me as the truck rumbles on through the night. It first occurred to me when I was loading cartons. I attempted to dismiss it, to slap it away. But it is the kind of thought that is like a mosquito—once it has found you it keeps circling and trying to land, and as I sit in the dark truck I am defenseless against it.

Here is the thought: The man who is not my father is a mean man, but he is not a fool. He knows I hate his guts. He is far too smart to provide me with any ammunition I could ever use against him.

If he was involved in an illegal activity, he would keep it hidden from me. He would know that if I found out about it, I could tell my mother. I could even go to the police. We are sworn enemies, this man and I, and he is far too cunning to give his sworn enemy a powerful weapon to use against him.

Yet he has brought me along with him on this journey. This can mean only one of two things. It is possible that he means to silence me once and for all when our evening's work is concluded. This does not seem very likely, however. He is a mean and even a violent man, but I do not think he is the kind of cold-blooded killer who goes around murdering fourteen-year-old boys for borrowing some of his cash.

It is also possible that he has shown me his true colors, so to speak, because, for some reason that I cannot yet guess, he does not fear that I will retaliate. In other words, he has some powerful trump card yet to play before this night is over. He must know some reason why, even if he lets me go, I will never use this knowledge against him. I cannot imagine what this trump card could be, but even as I sit with my back to a row of cartons that seem ready to fall over at any second, I can guess that it is in some way connected to my mother, and her absence from our home that is not a home.

The truck finally stops. The back is opened, and I climb out. Our short haul has taken us to a ware-house. We may be near a port, because I smell the ocean, and, occasionally, I hear the throaty blasts of foghorns. The walls of the warehouse are concrete and the ceiling is at least thirty feet high. Thousands of boxes have been stacked along the sides to form several cardboard mountain chains. "Stack it all here," the short man says, pointing to some wooden pallets near the truck. "Let's go."

The same men we loaded the truck with begin to work. I cannot join them. My sore muscles and aching tendons have tightened up during the ride, so that I can barely walk, let alone bend over to help hoist a wide-screen TV set. I hesitate.

"Looks like your little leprechaun is all played out," the short man says to the man who is not my father with a laugh.

"No," the man who is not my father responds. "He'll work." And then he turns to me. His right hand shoots out and grabs a shock of my hair. I believe that for a second or two he actually lifts me off the ground, holding me by the hair. "You're only half done," he says.

It feels like the crown of my head is on fire. "Yes sir," I gasp. He lowers me back to earth, but I see that he is watching me and prepared to strike again if necessary. My brain immediately tries to rally the exhausted legionnaires in the near and far bivouacs of my body for one final campaign. It sounds the bugle call. "Arms, report for service. Legs, begin walking. We are in enemy territory. Left, right, left, right."

Slowly, tiredly, I find myself walking. Bending. Hoisting. Again and again. Ten minutes go by. Twenty minutes. Finally the last carton is unloaded from the truck and stacked on a wooden pallet.

The short man takes out a wad of cash. "Here's yours," he says to the man who is not my father. "And twenty for Shoeless Joe over there."

"Fifty," the man who is not my father says back to him.

"You're kidding, right? Thirty, and that's generous."

"Fifty, or we're gonna have trouble."

Everyone suddenly goes quiet. Apparently, these are not men who make idle threats. The word "trouble" buzzes in the air like an angry wasp at a picnic lunch. The short man looks back at the man who is not my father as if sizing him up. The man who is not my father returns his gaze steadily. I find myself wondering if the man who is not my father has taken his gun from his sock drawer and is carrying it in his pocket.

"Oh, take it and get the hell out of here," the short man finally says, peeling off several more bills and handing them to him.

The man who is not my father pockets the money and turns to me. "You know where to go," he says.

"Yes sir." I climb into the back of the truck. Without any TV sets, it feels spacious. The man who is not my father locks me in and gets in the cab, and off we go, just the two of us, speeding away into the dark and freezing night.

Our short haul is finished, but I sense that this strange night is not yet over.

16

trump card

We drive for a long time. I try to convince myself that we are heading home, and that I will soon be in my nice warm bed.

I am not sure what I will do if I suddenly find myself on my own street, in front of my home that is not a home. Perhaps I will scream for all the world to hear. Or perhaps I will run into the house, wake my mother, who is no doubt asleep, and tell her the truth about this man she has brought home to share my father's bed with. Or perhaps I will be craftier and bide my time until the moment is right to go to the police.

But in my heart of hearts, I must admit that I do not believe that we are heading home. I believe that the man who is not my father has other things planned. This entire strange night seems to be building toward some dramatic denouement, whatever that means. I do not know exactly how he intends to hurt me, but I have no doubt that that is his ultimate objective, and that he has something particularly excruciating planned.

In the darkness of the back of the truck, without even wide-screen TV sets for company, I can hear the beating of my own frightened heart. Ka-*thump*. Ka-*thump*. I find myself doing something that I rarely do—I whisper a prayer to my God who is not my God.

My God is not my God because he does not answer my prayers. Either he has no power, in which case he may be a very nice fellow but he is not a God, or he does not like me, in which case he may be a God but he is not *my* God. I have prayed to him many times and he has never once done what I ask him to do. In fact, he usually does almost exactly the opposite. Perhaps I should pray for what I do not want, and then I might get it.

"O God who is not my God," I pray, "you who have never granted even one of my extremely reasonable requests. You may wonder why I am praying to you, since we have such a bad track record together. Well, the simple fact is that I am all alone here in the back of this truck, and whether you are a God or not, and whether you even like me or not, you are all I have at the moment. You are it."

My prayer to my God who is not my God is not starting out very well, but I believe that honesty is the most important quality in a prayer, and I am doing the best I can. So I continue:

"Now, it is true that I have not led a perfect life. I admit that some of the thoughts that pop into my head are shameful and sinful and just plain outrageous, and if you can scan them over my shoulder, so to speak, I can imagine why you are disappointed in me. Furthermore, I know I have said on more than one occasion that I do not believe in you. But the truth is, O my God who is not my God, I did believe in you all along. I simply wasn't scared enough to admit it. Everybody believes in God if they are frightened enough, and right now I am feeling particularly faithful.

"But—and this is the most important thing, so please hear me out—I believe that deep down I am not such a bad person. I am not cruel. I do not hurt people without due cause. And I will try to be an even better person if you will just grant one very simple request: Get me out of here. Let me go home. Do not allow the man who is not my father to hurt me in whatever excruciating way he has planned. Show me some sign that you are with me, and that you have heard my prayer, and that you are prepared to act."

In the lonely silence of the back of the truck, I wait for some divine sign. It would be nice if a dove would perch on my shoulder. I would even settle for a moth landing on my nose. But if there is a sign, I do not detect it. We roll on through the night. And I am all alone in the darkness, listening to the beating of my own heart. Ka-*thump*. Ka-*thump*.

The truck slows and stops. The man who is not my father has brought me to the place of his choosing, and I sense a showdown is near.

I stand there, in the dark truck bed, and wonder where we are. We could be anywhere. We could be in some far corner of the universe. The way this particular night has been going, this would not surprise me at all.

The man who is not my father slides the door open. He is holding a flashlight in one hand. He shines it right in my eyes. This time he does not even need to say "Get out." I clamber down.

We are not in an alternate universe, but we are also not in front of my house that is not a house. We are in the middle of nowhere. Nowhere turns out to be cold and very dark. A night wind is blowing, and as I climb out of the truck with my sore legs and back protesting every movement, I believe the wind blows right through me.

We appear to be on the side of a narrow road in a forest. I can see bony tree limbs silhouetted overhead against the silvery moon. And I can hear the wind roaring between tree trunks and whistling through branches. If you do not think that wind can sound like a live animal—like a hungry and dangerous beast— then you have never been in a dark forest at night.

"You worked hard tonight," the man who is not my father says. "I'm proud of you."

I say nothing. I have no idea at all where this is going, except that I am very sure he is not proud of me in any way, shape, or form. He is setting me up. That's what he is doing.

"And I was proud that you didn't do something stupid, like try to make a run for it, or scream for help. That would have been a big mistake, and you were smart not to do it. You're clever that way. I

210

would have been very hard on you."

"You can stop threatening me," I tell him. "I did not scream and I did not run for it because you won't dare hurt me, and we both know it."

His flashlight beam is pointed at my face. I squint my eyes and look back at him—I can barely make out his features in the darkness. But I can hear his voice clearly, and he sounds almost amused as he asks, "Why do you think that?"

I play my only card. "My mom."

He laughs. "John, your mom is gone."

I have never been this cold in my life. My teeth are chattering so hard I can hardly talk. "Gone where?"

"Plenty too far to hear you scream. About five hundred miles. Her aunt is dying. I guess old Auntie Rose is all alone there, and your mom is the only person who can put her in the ground. She left this morning. Took the sick time she had saved up at the factory and caught the bus for Maysville."

For a moment, even in the bitter cold, I feel a pang of deep sympathy for a kind old woman I met only twice, years ago, when she visited us. Even then she was white-haired and frail, and she seemed all alone in the world.

"At first I didn't like it that your mom was going," the man who is not my father says. "She belongs home, taking care of me. I had some drinks and even tore up the house a little. But then I got to thinking. Maybe old Rose will leave us some money. I just hope your mom buries her cheap."

I have still not accepted the fact that my mother has deserted me. "I don't believe you," I blurt out. "She would never leave without even telling me."

"She didn't want her old aunt to die before she got there," the man who is not my father explains. "And I assured her that I would take the very best care of you till she got back. It could be two days. It could be a week. Who knows how much life old Rose has left in her." He pauses, and even though I cannot see his face clearly, I know the man who is not my father is giving me his cruel little smile. "And you're right— the fact is, your mom wanted to take you with her, but I convinced her it would be a mistake to pull you out of school. And we both agreed this would be a good opportunity."

The way he says this last word is very creepy. We are getting to the nitty-gritty. His trump card is in his hand, but he has not yet shown it to me.

"Opportunity for what?" I ask.

"For us to get used to our new relationship," the man who is not my father says.

I am afraid to hear what he will say next. He does not speak right away—he pauses for several seconds as if he is about to tell me something so unpleasant that it makes even him hesitate. "You see, John, the man who is your real father is coming back home. He should be there by tomorrow morning. I am moving out. There is no longer a place for me in your home. Your life will be happy now. I wanted to take you on a short haul tonight so that you could see exactly what I'm really like, and how miserable your life could have been if you hadn't caught this lucky break."

But, of course, the man who is not my father doesn't say any of this. This is the speech that I want to hear, but it is not the speech that he delivers. He just stands there, holding the flashlight in my eyes, and watches me shiver in the cold. Finally he speaks. "Your mother and I are getting married, John," he tells me. "As soon as she comes back from Maysville. Nothing fancy. Just a little wedding ceremony. Whatever old Rose leaves us will come in handy."

There is a roaring in my ears, and it has nothing to

do with the wind that is gusting around us.

"Well, aren't you going to say something?" he asks.

"Like what?"

"How about 'congratulations'?"

"Congratulations," I hear myself mutter.

For the first time he angles his flashlight so that I can see his own face. It is a face that I hate, from chin to hairline, from ear to ear. "Congratulations what?" he asks.

I shrug. What does it matter. "Congratulations, sir."

"No," he says, "congratulations, Father."

"That is something I will never say," I tell him. "Never in a million years. You can do whatever you want to me and I will never say it."

He smiles. "You look cold, John. I guess it's time to go home. We can talk about this some other time. We'll have lots of time to talk." And that is clearly a threat. I see now that everything he says and does is a trap or a land mine or carries a hidden threat. And the kinder or more honest he pretends to be, the more dangerous he really is. Now, looking at me, he appears almost sympathetic, and I prepare myself for the very worst. "But," he says in a low voice, "for what it's worth, even if you hate my guts, you should admit that I'm a better man than your real father ever was."

"*That's a lie,*" I say, much too loud. "You don't know my father. You don't know anything about him."

"Just what your mother's told me," he admits. "But that's enough. I never claimed to be a saint, John, but I would never have been cold enough to do what he did. To just leave a young wife and her little son, with no explanation and no forwarding address. To just disappear—drop off the face of the earth. That's beyond cruel. That's beyond heartless. Think what you will of me, John, even I would never do that. That's beyond contempt."

I open my mouth, but there is absolutely nothing I can say back to him. Instead, I feel tears in my eyes, and sobs in my throat, and I just lower my head in shame, because, God help me, what he has just said is true.

17

running away from home

You do not know me and you will not miss me.

I pack one bag. What a depressing yet thrilling realization—that all the items I value in life fit in one small black duffel bag.

The best time to run away from home is not the middle of the night. That is, in fact, one of the worst times you can try it. It is dark and cold in the middle of the night, and everyone who is not running away from home is asleep, so you will stand out. Police will spot you in bus stations. Passing motorists will not see you with your thumb out, or they will be too afraid to pick you up.

The best time is early in the morning, when the sun is just starting to come up, and everyone is busy brushing their teeth and getting dressed and the roads and bus stations and airports are starting to fill up with people in a hurry.

I am out on the road bright and early in my winter coat with my black duffel bag thrown over my shoulder. I am not cold because I am wearing long winter underwear under my jeans and flannel shirt. Zoom, zoom, the cars pass by, but I do not care. Eventually one will stop.

The day before, I wrote two letters. One was to the police, revealing all that I know of the man who is not my father's illegal activities. I mailed that letter yesterday afternoon, so they should be receiving it today at the station house. The other letter was to my mother, telling her that she has made her choice and now I am making mine. I left that letter in the top drawer of her dresser so that she will find it when she returns from burying her Aunt Rose.

Zoom, zoom, the cars go by.

And then one stops. It is a shiny red sports car, driven by a very attractive young woman. "Are you hitchhiking?" she asks me.

The question surprises me. "Don't you see my thumb sticking out?" I reply.

"But . . . you look like you should be in school."

"I won't ask you your business and please don't ask me mine," I respond. "I need a ride. Will you give me one?"

"Where are you going?" she asks.

"Where are *you* going?" I echo her question.

"Los Angeles," she says.

"That is where I am going, too."

She gives me a very long look. "You're determined to do this?"

"Yes," I say.

"You've considered all the options?"

"There are no options."

"Better me than somebody else," she says with a sigh. "Get in."

We drive across the vast United States together. We cross prairies. We see muskrats. We cross mountains. We see bighorn sheep. We cross rivers. We see barges and riverboats. This is a great big beautiful country, the United States. The man who is not my father will never find me. The police in my town that is not a town will find him, but they, too, will never find me. My mother will never locate me.

I am free and clear.

The woman's name turns out to be Miranda. In

the early afternoon of one sunny day we stop to eat lunch at a rest stop on a mountain overlooking a prairie. I violate my own rule and ask her about her business. "Why are you going to Los Angeles?"

"I live in Los Angeles," Miranda says. "I am returning home."

"What do you do there?"

"I run a school for girls," she says. "It is not a big school, but it is a very special school. The student body consists of two hundred teenage girls. And did I mention that all the teachers are women, too. My school is right on the beach. It is called the Los Angeles Girls School on the Beach. If you don't have a place to stay in Los Angeles, John, why don't you come and stay at the school for a while."

"What would I do at the school?" I ask.

"You could be a lifeguard at the giant Jacuzzi," she says. "And you could rub suntan oil on the girls when they start to get sunburned . . ."

As you have probably guessed by now, I am not in fact running away from home. If I did run away from home, the odds are very strong that I would not be picked up by a beautiful woman like Miranda. The odds are I would be picked up by a nutcase or a robber or a child molester. But that is not why I don't run away from home.

I do not run away from home because that would be surrender. I am pretty far down, but I am not yet out. I am currently lying on my bed. It is Monday, a school day, but I am not at school. This morning I prepared breakfast for the man who is not my father, as I did on Saturday morning, and again on Sunday morning, according to his instructions. I fetched his newspaper. I brewed his coffee. I called him sir.

I did not know that it was possible for me to hate someone as much as I hate him.

My body is not as sore as it was on Saturday morning, when I could barely get out of bed, but it is still sore. "I am not going to school today," I told the man who is not my father when he finished his breakfast this morning. "I am sick."

"What's wrong with you?" he asked.

"I'm still sore from Friday night."

He looked at me over the top of his newspaper, and his eyes narrowed dangerously. "Nothing happened on Friday night and you'll keep your mouth shut."

"Yes, but I don't feel good."

"Then don't go to school. What do I care. But

you'll go tomorrow, no matter how you feel. Got that?"

"Yes sir."

The man who is not my father drove away in his truck after breakfast and I am lying in my bed thinking about running away from home, and how I will never do it. I will not do it because I will not surrender to the man who is not my father. But there is another reason why I will never do it. I cannot possibly run away from home because I do not have a home to run away from. My home is not a home—it is enemy territory. You cannot run away from something that you do not have.

The man who is not my father has his own theories about family, some of which he was kind enough to set forth for my benefit on the ride home from the forest on Friday night. I admit I do not remember that ride very well. I was shivering with cold and misery, and I spent at least the first hour of that ride trying to stop crying without much success.

"Oh, stop your blubbering," the man who is not my father said several times with his usual sympathy. "You think you've been dealt a hard hand just because your father ditched you, and now you've got me to deal with. Well, let me tell you something, everyone takes their lumps. Did I ever tell you about Mona?"

I do not remember signifying any interest in the subject, but the man who is not my father plowed ahead with his peculiar variation of a father-to-son pep talk.

"Mona was my angel. There was never anyone like Mona. I look at your cow of a mother, and I think of my Mona, and it makes me ready to puke. We were made for each other, Mona and I. You have no idea, John. You'll never have an idea. Love like that is only given to a few people, and you're not the kind who's going to ever risk enough to find it. The day I married Mona was the happiest day of my life. I thought I had died and gone to heaven, and she was my reward. We spent three years together. We had a great house and I was raking in the bucks, and it was made in the shade—"

The man who is not my father broke off.

I saw a small opportunity to cause him pain and, of course, I seized it. "I always thought she died in a car accident," I said. And then I asked him, "What happened to Mona?"

He did not answer right away, but I believe his fingers squeezed a half inch into the hard plastic of the steering wheel. "What happened?" he finally repeated. "I took my lumps, that's what happened. She was like your father—cold as ice. She met a man who owned a car dealership and he flashed some cash at her. That was the car accident. If I ever meet him, he'll regret he was ever born. So she left me, and I did a little drinking and I lost the house and I pretty well flushed myself down the toilet, and here we are all in the septic tank together," the man who is not my father said with a bitter laugh, finishing off with the kind of vulgar image he is particularly good at constructing.

He drove the big truck for a few minutes in silence. "But my point is, John," he finally said, "that I took my lumps. And your mother is the best I can do now. And your mother took her lumps. Frankly, Johnny boy, you were one of those lumps she got stuck with. But that wasn't your fault. And, I grant you, you've taken some lumps yourself. So we're all here in the septic tank together and we'll just have to make the best of it. And if having me as a father doesn't sit too well with you, look on the bright side. You're already in high school. Pretty soon you'll be out in the world, and you can go wherever you like and do whatever you damn well please."

That, as far as I can remember it, was the man who is not my father's pep talk to me as we drove home from the forest. I am sorry to report that it did not fill me with hope or make me feel very much better, but I don't believe that was its point. I believe the central message and purpose of the pep talk was to let me know that I am now the expendable member of the family, so to speak, and I should set my sights on the open road.

I also believe I understand why the man who is not my father allowed me to ride back from the forest in the front seat of the truck, next to him. He kept me locked in the back so that I did not see any places by which I could identify the basement garage or the warehouse. He is not a stupid man, this man who is not my father. Just in case I do try to go to the police, he has made very sure that I have nothing to tell them. I do not even know in what state the loading and unloading of the TV sets took place.

I have no evidence. It would be my word against his. And he is my new stepdad, whom I clearly hate.

The man who is not my father is a very devious man, and he has got me right where he wants me.

I have also, in the past two days, had two brief conversations with my mother. She is apparently practically living at the hospital, where her aunt slips in and out of consciousness. Both times she phoned home in the evening, at a prearranged time, and the man who is not my father stood five feet away and listened to every word of my two brief and stilted conversations with her.

"How are you, John?" she asked, the first time she called. As if she cared!

I heard my voice answer her back, cold and flat. "Fine."

"I'm so sorry I didn't get to say goodbye, but I needed to leave right away. I hope you understand it was an emergency."

"Yeah."

"Aunt Rose has been fighting hard, but it doesn't look good. I had to be here with her."

"Sure."

"How's school?"

"Okay."

"And band? Are you practicing your tuba?"

"Sure."

"You're not saying much, John. Is everything okay?"

I glanced at the man who is not my father. He was standing close enough so that I could smell his breath. "Sure," I said, "everything's fine."

I heard her hesitate. "Did you hear the big news?"

"Yes."

"I wanted to tell you myself. But we can talk about it when I get back. It'll be great. You'll see. We'll be a family together."

"Sure," I say, so elated with the prospect that I nearly take a bite out of the phone. "Congratulations."

"You two are getting along okay?"

"Sure. I'll put him back on. He's right here. Bye."

I am sad to report that my phone conversations with my mother also did not fill me with hope or make me feel better about my life.

It is now noon on Monday. Tomorrow I must go to school and face Mrs. Moonface and somehow explain away a whole weekend's worth of algebra homework that I did not do. Also, I believe that Billy Beezer is probably back in school, and we may still be in a state

226

of war. Finally, Mr. Steenwilly will expect me to have made significant progress on my tuba solo, when the truth is that my tuba has been hibernating at the bottom of my closet, which I believe it thinks is a pond.

My closet may indeed be a pond, because it is certainly not a clothes closet. It is not a clothes closet, because there are virtually no clothes in it. All my good clothes were left in Glory Hallelujah's basement when our brief snuggle on her couch ended so abruptly. Perhaps they have been seized by the police as evidence.

I have not seen Gloria or talked to her since I followed D.D. out the pet door, and it is not a comforting thought that tomorrow Gloria and I will be reunited to discuss our romantic past, present, and future.

Let me state for the record that I do not want to go to anti-school tomorrow. But I also do not want to stay in my home that is not a home. I cannot run away from home because that would be a surrender, and, anyway, I do not have a home to run away from. I therefore also cannot drive away with Miranda, which is okay because she does not exist.

You do not know me, so you can't possibly know how trapped I feel. I am not trapped in a truck, or locked in a room. I am trapped in the worst kind of trap a fourteen-year-old boy can be trapped in—I am trapped inside my life that is not a life.

So I lie here in my bed, for hour after hour, looking up at the spidery cracks on the white ceiling.

18

fateful Tuesday begins

It is Tuesday, fateful Tuesday, and I am standing on the third floor of my anti-school, in front of my locker, issuing threats.

I have dialed the correct combination. I have turned the knob three to the left, four to the right, five to the left. I have pulled the handle gently, and then more firmly, and then with all my strength.

But the door has not opened. It has not even attempted to open. If anything, it is now locked more securely than when I dialed the combination. In fact, I have never seen a locker door, or any other kind of door for that matter, settle itself so resolutely into its frame and grasp its own hinges as if hunkering down for a long Russian winter.

My locker does not have a mouth, so it cannot speak, but it is thinking, "Begone, dorkheimer. You have no power here anymore. You, who call the man who is not your father sir, who cannot even run away from home because you don't have a home to run away from—I will never again open for the likes of you."

Homeroom will start soon, and I am running out of time and patience. I lift up my boot. "Do you see this?" I ask my locker door. "Are you by any chance acquainted with the words 'steel toe'? Or do the words 'permanent dent' mean anything to you?"

My locker door is not intimidated. "My grandfather was a vault at Fort Knox, and if you try to dent me with a kick you will only tear some ligament that will never mend."

I draw back my right leg to give my locker door a good swift kick. I believe I do manage to put a small dent in it, or at least nick off a bit of blue paint, but my locker door fights back. It reaches out, grabs my right boot by the heel, and with a jujitsu move flips me over onto my back. I was not expecting a counterattack, and I believe that as I fall I let out a loud scream.

From my supine position on the hallway floor I see several of my fellow students staring at me, and I believe I hear a few unkind guffaws. I give them back the old dead-fish gaze. "Do not stare at me like that, because you are merely wasting your time. I am already a dead flounder lying on the dock waiting to be scaled. Since I am brain-dead and my sensory nervous system has long since been switched off, I cannot suffer anymore. Save your stares and laughs for those still capable of registering shame and feeling pain."

I slowly stand up, my right leg, knee, and foot throbbing like they will all have to be amputated by the school nurse at the earliest opportunity, and only then, out of the corner of my eye, do I see that Glory Hallelujah has walked up, and is standing less than three feet away.

She is wearing a light blue sweater that looks so soft I believe it may actually be made of cotton candy. Her lovely blond hair falls gently about her shoulders, like the boughs of a weeping willow tree upon a grassy riverbank on a midsummer morning. But her blue eyes, which are focused on me, are not twinkling like warm stars. I am sorry to say they are glittering like cold dagger points.

"Hi," I say. "I was just practicing a soccer move."

Gloria does not say anything, but I believe her face

reflects doubt that what she just witnessed has ever intentionally been tried on any soccer field by any player since that globally popular game was invented.

When the silence stretches beyond the awkward point, I fracture it with another conversational salvo from my ineffective arsenal, whatever that means. "I kind of need the stuff I left at your house," I tell Gloria.

Once again, she does not reply, but in addition to anger, her face shows just a bit of confusion. I believe she has no idea at all what stuff I am talking about.

"My sweater, my shoes, and especially my jacket," I explain. "I left them right by the couch."

Her lovely lips part, and I see that she is now preparing to join our conversation. "And that's what you have to say to me?" she asks in a voice so cold that I believe her vocal cords must be lubricated with antifreeze or they would snap apart.

I do not know how to answer this question, so I nod.

"You have a lot of nerve," Glory Hallelujah tells me. "That stuff's gone."

"Gone where?" I ask.

"My father took it. I think he burned it."

I think of my green Christmas sweater and my good tan jacket going up in flames while the Bulldozer squirts more lighter fluid on them. "But . . . those things belonged to me," I point out in my humblest and most reasonable tone.

"If you wanted them so badly, maybe you shouldn't have left them there," she replies.

I do not want to argue with Gloria on fateful Tuesday, but I cannot resist pointing out, "I did not want to leave them there, but I did not have much choice. I had to leave in a hurry."

Her blue eyes get even colder. I believe they are now twin icicle points glittering in the polar sun. "You had a choice," she says. "You could have stayed and faced the music. I stayed—you could have stayed. Instead you ran."

My locker attempts to join the discussion. It cannot speak, because it does not have a mouth, but what it is trying to say to Gloria is: "You are absolutely right. He is a pathetic coward, and you are wasting your time with a dorkheimer like him. Blow him off, and let's go get a cup of coffee."

I will deal with my locker later. There is a hacksaw in the shop room. I focus my attention on Gloria. "Of course you stayed—you live there. But I didn't have a choice. Your father was going to kill me. And I need those clothes. Especially my jacket. There was some money in the pocket."

Gloria steps forward. I have never seen so much anger in such a pretty face before. It is like a hailstorm on a bright spring day. "So you're worried about a little money that you lost?" she asks. She is now rather close to me. That would normally be a pleasant thing, but on this particular morning Gloria is not in a friendly mood. Indeed, I believe she could spit venom like a cobra.

Her voice drops down to what I would call a whisper, except that the word "whisper" implies a soft quality, and there is nothing soft about the questions she suddenly fires off at me like quick pistol shots. "John, do you have any idea the amount of trouble you caused me?" she demands. "What could I say when you ran off? What could I tell the police? What could I say to our neighbors who came by to see if anything was wrong?"

"I'm very sorry you had to go through that," I say. "But, Gloria, I did not create the situation."

"Oh, like I did?" she asks. "Like I carried you down

there against your will. I can see you're great at taking responsibility. Do you have any idea what my parents did to me?" She hesitates, for dramatic effect. Her pearly teeth clench and unclench. "I was grounded for the whole weekend," she finally announces, as if she has spent twenty years in solitary confinement on Devil's Island. "I missed the Victoria Challenge Cup. Mindy Fairchild rode Luke all through the show because I wasn't there. And she won a blue ribbon. There's a picture of her and Luke hanging up at the stable now."

I briefly consider Gloria's punishments and misfortunes, holding them up next to my own, and I decide that fate has let her off rather easily. "Well, I suffered a bit, too," I tell her. "It hasn't been easy for me either. Okay?"

Glory Hallelujah—how is it possible for your pupils to flash like warning lights, and for your adorable nostrils to flare so violently they almost rip your nose apart, and for you to draw yourself up like a Roman emperor about to declare war on some hapless province? And since we are having a private conversation, why is your voice rising from a low level till it now fills the entire hallway?

"DON'T YOU EVER SPEAK TO ME AGAIN," Glory Hallelujah commands. "DON'T PASS ME ANY OF YOUR STUPID NOTES. AND DON'T TELL ME ANY MORE OF YOUR DISGUSTING LIES."

We are attracting quite a bit of attention. Surely the students now gawking at us will leave their lockers and go to their homerooms to give us some privacy.

"What lies?" I ask.

"YOU'RE NOT ON THE SOCCER TEAM! I ASKED GARY CAMPBELL, THE CAPTAIN. HE JUST LAUGHED. HE SAID IF YOU TRIED OUT FOR THE SOCCER TEAM, THEY WOULDN'T EVEN LET YOU WIPE THE MUD OFF THEIR SHOES!"

It occurs to me that the captain of the soccer team is probably stretching the truth a bit. I believe that if I tried out for the team, they would indeed allow me to wipe the mud from their shoes. But I hesitate to point this out to Gloria, because her face is flushed and her voice is now so loud that I believe it can probably be heard all through our anti-school, from the French lab on the fourth floor to the boiler room in the sub-basement. "MY FATHER WAS RIGHT ABOUT YOU!" she shouts, pointing at me with her right hand. "YOU'RE A FAKE AND A PHONY! BUT NOW I KNOW EXACTLY WHO AND WHAT YOU ARE. YOU'RE JUST A LITTLE COWARD AND A LIAR!"

There are gasps and some scattered applause from several dozen of my locker neighbors, who are apparently willing to risk detention to see the end of my little encounter with the prettiest girl in our anti-school.

I look back into those beautiful blue eyes that I have spent so much time dreaming about. "No, Gloria, you're wrong," I hear myself say. I don't know where I get the courage, but I am looking right back at her, and I believe my own eyes may be flashing just a bit. "You see, I don't know who you are." My voice is getting louder, too, and she actually takes a half step backward as I proclaim the truth, loud enough for all in the hallway to hear: "AND YOU DON'T KNOW ME. WE WENT OUT ON ONE LOUSY DATE. YOU DON'T KNOW ME AT ALL."

"Fine. Let's keep it that way," she says, turns on her heel, and walks quickly away.

19

fateful Tuesday picks
up steam

There are five minutes to go in anti-math class, and I am trying to survive a triple threat. Death lasers are being aimed at me from two directions, from Billy Beezer on my left and Glory Hallelujah on my right. If I were to duck suddenly, they would be firing right at each other.

Meanwhile, in the front of the room, Mrs. Moonface is in rare form. She has wrapped up the unit on mixture equations, and moved on to the next subject in her algebra gibberish curriculum. She has spent the entire period lecturing on a new species of mathematical mystery called Linear Systems in Two Variables. She has filled up a world-record three entire blackboards with rules, examples, and solutions for graphing and unraveling these profound puzzles.

She is now waving a rather large piece of chalk around, like a pioneer trying to fend off a bear with a bowie knife, and saying, "So, I hope you all now see that solving a system of equations consists of finding all the ordered pairs, if any, which satisfy each of the equations in the system."

No, Mrs. Moonface, I do not see that at all. What I see is that you waited all weekend for a handsome man named Jacques sporting a polka-dot bow tie to show up at your door and take you swing dancing. He never showed up, so you have decided to suck up all the disappointment, loneliness, and misery you feel, meld it in your mind as if in a trash compactor into a fifty-minute algebra lesson from hell, and spew it back at us in the form of indecipherable graphs and incomprehensible equations so cumulatively toxic that I believe they could corrode vulcanized steel. You have just glanced at the clock, and I believe you are at this very moment composing a death question to winnow out at least one member of my anti-math class before our period ends.

Mrs. Moonface, today I have more urgent worries. There are forces at work against me in this class even more deadly than algebra. I believe at any second my textbook will catch fire from the laser beams flashing at me from Glory Hallelujah's blue eyes and the ion blasts directed at me from Billy Beezer's nose cannon.

My friend who is not a friend and I exchanged our first words since his basketball game arrest just before this math class began, and, it pains me to report, they were not filled with warmth and friendship. Among the Lashasa Palulu, when two young men are feuding and one is willing to put the ill will to rest, it is considered good manners and wise policy for him to approach his enemy with respectful formality, and to speak about matters such as the weather that are banal, whatever that means, and that cannot possibly give offense. "Good morning, William Beanman," I said as we walked into the room and sat down side by side. "And how are you on this gray Tuesday?"

He did not reply to this first conversational salvo, except to grind his teeth together with sufficient force so that the muscles of his mandible stood out.

"I thought it might snow, but now it looks like rain," I continued. "Or it could hail, or even perhaps sleet." Having exhausted all the main meteorological possibilities, I sat back in my chair and waited for his response.

"You're dead meat," my friend who is not a friend

finally spat back in my direction. "Dead meat, do you hear? You're carrion."

No one had ever called me carrion before, and I found I did not enjoy the experience. "Strong words from a two-time felon," I told him. "You really must reform, forgive, and forget, or you may end up on death row."

That was the extent of our conversation. But throughout the period, at well-spaced intervals, Billy Beezer has whispered ominously at me, "Dead meat, dead meat." And on several of the many occasions when Mrs. Moonface has turned away from us to fill her three blackboards with algebraic hieroglyphics, Billy Beezer has physically assaulted me with several of the mathematical learning aids that the Beezer parents have generously purchased for their son's edification. He jabbed me with a slide rule. He poked me with a protractor. He stabbed me with the point of his compass hard enough to break my skin and draw blood.

Mrs. Moonface, I believe the Board of Education has entrusted you with a clear responsibility to prevent your students from being stabbed with mathematical learning aids during your class. But instead of your protecting the innocent, your eyes are now gleaming with an eager sadistic pleasure. "I see that we still have five minutes left in the period," you observe, putting down the chalk and rubbing your hands together. "Let us explore the practical applications of solving two variable linear equations by looking at one very simple question. Who would like to volunteer?"

Mrs. Moonface waits expectantly for volunteers. She manages to convey in her attitude that any student raising his or her hand will be performing an act of selfless bravery that may rescue the rest of the platoon. If this were a war movie, a fresh-faced private from middle America would step forward and volunteer for the suicide mission. "Sarge," he would say, "choose me. I'm your man to walk through this minefield and take out the machine gun nest." But this is not a war movie—this is anti-math class, and we are all hunkered down in our anti-algebra shelters waiting for the bombing raid to pass.

When it becomes clear that no one is dumb enough to take on her death question voluntarily, Mrs. Moonface begins searching for a live victim. "Then I suppose I'll have to choose," she says with obvious relish. "Let's see. Who haven't we heard from in a while?"

Her eyes do a quick death scan around the room, sweeping over the rows of students. Everyone goes into survival mode. For a long moment her gaze settles on Norman Cough, but he cleverly extricates himself by a short bronchial blast of such concentrated lung power that it moves his entire desk several feet to his right, much the way the deep-sea octopus escapes predators by sudden bursts of water from its mantle cavity.

Mrs. Moonface appears momentarily confused—Norman was in Row A but he is suddenly in Row C. She could try to pin him down again, at his new location, but he is looking back at her confidently, as if to say, "Mrs. Moonface, I am far too elusive a foe for the likes of you on this Tuesday morning. I am completely capable of coughing myself around this room for the next four minutes and forty-eight seconds if necessary."

Mrs. Moonface goes off in search of less mobile prey. She next focuses her death gaze on Karen Dirigible's desk. A large purple poster advertising Open School Night has been tacked up on the bulletin board behind Karen's desk, and she has dressed in careful camouflage to take advantage of this backdrop. This morning she is wearing a purple dress that so perfectly matches the poster that one can look directly at her and not see any sign of an algebra student whatsoever.

Mrs. Moonface pauses. She knows from the attendance sheet that Karen must be at the end of Row A, so she peers one way and then another, narrows her eyes, and walks several steps to one side for a better angle, but Karen Dirigible is like a sand crab on a dune—a predator can look directly at her and see nothing that can be eaten.

Mrs. Moonface's death gaze sweeps on to me. Now, as I have demonstrated before, I am a master at avoiding unwanted algebra questions and there are several advanced techniques I could employ if necessary. But the truth is, there are now only four minutes and seven seconds left in the period. It will take Mrs. Moonface at least ten seconds to ask her question. I am quite capable of stalling for four minutes, neither answering nor not answering, till the period comes to an end. So I look directly back at Mrs. Moonface. "Do not call on me," I am saying to her, "because you will be wrestling a cloud."

"John," she says, taking up my challenge, "I haven't called your name in a while. Here is a very simple double variable question. An auto parts store ordered a combined total of fifty cases of oil filters and air cleaners that cost a total of three thousand two hundred and eleven dollars and eighty cents. Each case of oil filters costs seventy dollars and seventy cents and each case of air cleaners costs thirty dollars and thirty cents. How many cases of oil filters and how many cases of air cleaners were ordered?"

There is silence in the class. The death question has been let out of its box. It uncurls itself like a giant scorpion and approaches me, its cold arachnid eyes measuring me while its sensory bristles twitch menacingly.

I am remarkably calm. Mrs. Moonface, in asking me this death question you wasted seventeen precious seconds. That leaves me with a mere three minutes and fifty seconds of stall time—a piece of cake for an advanced practitioner of question avoidance such as myself.

I begin with the old ear pull. No, Mrs. Moonface, do not be tricked by my tugging at my earlobe into thinking that I am actually considering your question. The truth is that I do not have the slightest notion how many oil filters and air cleaners the auto parts store ordered, nor do I have the faintest glimmer of an idea of how those two variables could be solved. In fact, no one in this entire anti-math class has even a prayer of ever solving your problem, and I believe that even Albert Einstein at age fourteen, on a good day, would not have stood much of a chance.

Furthermore, Mrs. Moonface, although you claim this is a practical question, I believe there is not an auto parts store in the entire known universe that buys its oil filters and air cleaners with such sophisticated mathematical techniques. It is my firm belief that in most auto parts stores they buy enough oil filters and air cleaners to fill their shelf space, and when those run out someone says, "Hey, Joe, better order a few more of those air cleaners. And throw in some more oil filters, too."

I am sorry to report, Mrs. Moonface, that my earlobe tugging has absolutely nothing to do with actual thought. Its devious twin purposes are movement and distraction—I am simulating thought. And since the old earlobe pull has worked so well for twenty seconds, I am now adding the old brow wrinkle as well. Do not think, Mrs. Moonface, that the furrows and creases now appearing and disappearing across my brow and forehead indicate any cerebral activity taking place inside my cranium. You cannot judge a book by its cover, Mrs. Moonface, and you also cannot judge brain function or lack thereof by superficial forehead furrowing.

"John, are you making any progress?"

Yes, indeed, Mrs. Moonface, I have just made fifty seconds of progress in stalling out your death question. There are a mere three minutes remaining. That is less time than it takes a world-class runner to run a mile. It is also less time, Mrs. Moonface, than it takes to cook three one-minute eggs back to back. You will not get an answer today, Mrs. Moonface, but you also will not not get an answer. You are wrestling vapor. You are punching snowflakes.

"This question is kicking your butt, doofus," Billy Beezer taunts me in a subsonic whisper. "You're dead meat. Dead meat."

It is regrettable that my algebra-class neighbor is so negative, but his comments do not faze me. I am also not getting much encouragement from the other direction. On my right side, Glory Hallelujah sits forward and squints her eyes at me, amping up the firepower of her death lasers so that I believe the legs of my desk begin to melt. She is looking right at me, her two bright blue eyes flashing with fearful intensity.

I decided not to send up any friendly conversational flares in Glory Hallelujah's direction before this anti-math class began. As you may remember, she vowed in the hall this morning that she and I would never speak again, and third period seemed to me a bit soon to put her oath to the test. Several times this morning we have bumped into each other in the school hallways, and she has shown no sign whatsoever of wanting to bury the hatchet, so to speak.

As Gloria and I passed each other in the hall between first and second periods, I saw her chatting with two of her friends, Yuki Kaguchi and Julie Moskowitz, both charter members of the secret sorority of pretty fourteen-year-old girls. As I walked by, Gloria pointed me out to them with a rather rude hand gesture, and began to whisper furiously.

I hesitate to speculate without the facts, but I believe that Gloria was spreading certain negative reports about me, as dating material, to her friends. She was, perhaps, telling them that I am a liar, a coward, and even a bad kisser who nips noses and then flees irate fathers. I believe it is eminently possible that a worldwide emergency bulletin has gone out to all members of the secret sorority of pretty fourteen-year-old girls that I am never again to be dated under any circumstances. And now, having ruined my romantic chances for the rest of my life, Gloria is concentrating her ocular-based laser attack in an effort to finish me off once and for all. I can feel the heat from her angry blue eyes singeing the delicate hairs on my forearms.

"John," Mrs. Moonface asks, "are the wheels turning? Do you at least have a first step in mind?"

Yes, Mrs. Moonface, the first step I have in mind is right out the door. In two minutes and twenty-seven seconds, when the bell rings, let me assure you that I will be the very first member of this anti-math class out that door. You will not see me leave, because I will be traveling at the speed of light, but I will be gone.

Since the old earlobe pull and forehead furrow are starting to wear thin, and we are closing in on our final two-minute countdown, I decide to enhance my stall with some appropriate sound effects. Looking directly back at Mrs. Moonface, I clear my throat as if I am about to utter some profound mathematical observation that is at the very tip of my tongue. "Uh-ghh-huh," I grunt, nodding my head slightly. "Un-nuhh-hah. Uwha-nn-hmm."

I see that you have been completely taken in by the old throat clearings, Mrs. Moonface. You are leaning forward, as if you believe I am at the brink of declaiming some deep mathematical epiphany, whatever that means. You do not realize that those are actually the very same throat-clearing sounds I made last spring when a fly flew into my mouth and became wedged in my esophagus.

"John, are you trying to work it all out in your head? Have you formed the system to be solved? Take it step by step, John. Have you even defined your variables?"

There is less than one minute to go! Mrs. Moonface is launching questions at me, but I am firing back at her on all cylinders. I am pulling the old earlobe so hard that it is almost stretched beneath my chin. My brow and forehead are furrowing and unfurrowing so rapidly and deeply that my eyebrows are in danger of becoming unstitched and peeling off my face. I am rocking back and forth in my seat as if I can barely contain my excitement at wrestling with this algebraic enigma. And every five or ten seconds I am dredging up a new throat-clearing sound for Mrs. Moonface, as if I am at the very brink of explicating a mathematical insight that will shake the foundations of modern number theory.

"John, we're running out of time."

"Yes, indeed we are, Mrs. Moonface."

"What did you say?"

"Nice try, Mrs. Moonface, but you will not trick me into blurting out a wrong answer by pretending that I have begun to try to solve a problem that I have absolutely no intention of ever trying to solve. Mrs. Moonface, you may be so miserable in your own pathetic life that you have to try to stump us with these algebra questions from the lowest level of hell and make fools of us, and destroy our self-esteem, but that doesn't mean that I plan to give in one iota to your need for self-gratification by sadistic algebra torture of the innocent . . ."

At this moment, I become aware that the class is

roaring with laughter. I also observe that Mrs. Moonface's face—always the pasty color of the lunar surface—has turned the bleached color, granular texture, and, I suspect, bitter taste of salt. She lets out something that is halfway between a sigh and a scream, and leans heavily against her desk.

I realize to my horror that the little man in the swivel chair has made a major, horrific mistake at the control board of my brain. Blinded by lasers from the girl of my dreams and befuddled by ion bursts from my friend who is not a friend; riddled with anger toward my mother and seething with fury toward the man who is not and never will be my father; confounded by an algebra question that has pincerlike claws and a hollow, poisonous stinger; and lost without a compass amid a sea of troubles in my life that is not a life, I have actually been speaking my thoughts out loud! I have called Mrs. Moonface Mrs. Moonface to her face!

The whole class is laughing. And now the kinder members of the class have begun to stop laughing because poor old Mrs. Gabriel is hyperventilating . . . and her fingers are shaking . . .

And then the bell rings. Algebra class is over. I rise

and begin to exit the room at the speed of light, but I am not the first person out the door. Mrs. Moonface beats me into the hallway. The last I see of her, she is sprinting toward the ladies' faculty bathroom, making sounds as if she is drowning, and she is covering her face with her hands.

fateful Tuesday reaches a crescendo

"Dear, dear members of the band family," Mr. Steenwilly says to us, and his nervousness is very apparent in every word and every fidgety gesture, "I know that you have all been working on 'The Love Song of the Bullfrog' as hard as you can, practicing it night and day. I'm sure I don't have to remind you that our Winter Concert—the world premiere of this, my finest composition—is now only two weeks away. But today we have a chance to have a little world premiere before the big world premiere! This is a very special day!"

Mr. Steenwilly pauses. Do not look in my direction, Mr. Steenwilly. This is indeed a very special day, but for all the wrong reasons. It is fateful Tuesday, and anything I touch crumbles to dust. Look away out the window of the band room, or down at the tips of your loafers, but do not train those excited black eyes in my direction.

"Today we have a guest," Mr. Steenwilly announces. "A very special guest. A celebrity guest! None other than Professor Gustav Slavodan Kachooski—my old instructor and mentor from the Eastman School of Music and, in the minds of many, one of the foremost musicologists ever to draw breath! He stopped by our school to pay me a surprise visit today, and he has agreed to stay and hear you play!" Mr. Steenwilly glances toward the band office. "This is a great honor," he says with awe sloshing around thickly in his voice, like suds in a washing machine. "Truly a great honor. Please, Professor."

A short, bald old man in a dark suit walks out of the band office blowing his nose in a long continuous honk, in what I believe is a B flat. He finally tucks his handkerchief into a back pocket, arranges his black-framed eyeglasses on the bridge of his small nose, and says, "Please, Arthur, you're too kind, too kind. The honor is all mine, all mine, to hear my best student's best students."

Professor Kachooski, if you are really one of the

foremost musicologists ever to draw breath, you might want to run out of this anti-school while you can still respirate. Mr. Steenwilly, if I may also take the liberty of giving you a piece of advice which you would be very wise to follow, you should probably drag your old professor back into the band office and fix him a nice cup of Earl Grey tea with low-fat milk, and reminisce about your halcyon days together at the music academy, whatever that means.

But, Mr. Steenwilly, if you insist on going forward with this ill-advised surprise concert, I think it might be prudent for you to let Kachooski know that the tuba soloist he is about to hear is in the midst of a personal meltdown on the level of the Chernobyl reactor, and that on this fateful Tuesday I could not play "Mary Had a Little Lamb," let alone "The Love Song of the Bullfrog."

Mr. Steenwilly sets up a folding chair for Professor Kachooski so that the old man will have a good visual and aural vantage point for the upcoming performance. "Closer," Kachooski says to him, "let me sit closer, Arthur. I don't want to miss a single brilliant note."

Kachooski, you are asking for it, and I fear that you

are going to get it. I do not mean to be pessimistic about the quality of the musical rendition you are about to hear, but if I were you, I would take out that white handkerchief and stuff it deep into your ears.

Mr. Steenwilly climbs onto his conducting podium and looks out at us. His thin mustache quivers above his lip line, as if it is so overcome with the poignancy of the moment that it is tempted to slither off his face and hide in the collar of his starched white shirt. "May I just say," he tells us, with a nervous little grin, "that at the Eastman School of Music, Professor Kachooski had a nickname. We called him 'the Man with the Golden Ear.' And now that golden ear is going to hear some golden notes from all of you."

Kachooski sits back in his folding chair and smiles at us. He does not realize that "the Man with the Golden Ear" is about to meet "the Boy with the Frog for a Tuba," and that that is likely to be a pairing similar to "Shirley Temple Meets the Bride of Dracula."

"And now," Mr. Steenwilly says, with one last nervous glance back at Kachooski, " 'The Love Song of the Bullfrog.' "

Down sweeps the arm that holds the baton. Violent Hayes begins to play the opening interlude.

The monitor lizard that is pretending to be her saxophone must be intimidated by Kachooski's presence, because it gives off no reptilian screeches. On the contrary, it lies quietly in her arms and does a very good imitation of a saxophone being well played by a serious high school music student who has practiced long and hard and is concentrating with every brain cell at her command. Violent Hayes is nailing the opening interlude.

On his podium, Mr. Steenwilly smiles at her, and the ends of his mustache appear to be tap-dancing on the points of his cheekbones with joy and pride. On his folding chair, Professor Kachooski is all smiles, his head cocked slightly to one side so that his golden ear can suck up every sharp and flat in the Steenwilly opus.

As the saxophone interlude comes to an end, Andy Pearce lets loose with a percussive riff on the old drums. Now, normally when Andy Pearce plays the drums, it sounds like a traffic accident between several large vehicles traveling at high speeds in opposite directions. But on this day there must be a good traffic cop at the intersection, because Andy Pearce plays smoothly and flawlessly.

Mr. Steenwilly's black eyes pop out of his head triumphantly, like corks out of a champagne bottle. Kachooski is nodding and pursing his lips thoughtfully, as if to say, "Well done, Steenwilly. You took on a crusade and you have spread light to this anti-school. Well done."

I myself have no time to enjoy the music. My tuba solo is crawling toward me through the musical bars like a saltwater crocodile with its giant razor-toothed mouth agape.

I consider faking a heart attack. I attempt to levitate myself out the band room door, but I do not manage to raise myself even a half inch above the well-worn band shell floor. I consider the odds that lightning will strike my anti-school out of a clear sky in the next twelve seconds, or that an alien invasion launched light-years ago in some dark corner of the universe may reach the planet Earth before my tuba solo arrives. Neither of these seems like a strong possibility.

Meanwhile, the frog that pretends to be my tuba evinces no signs of life whatsoever. I believe a fossilized frog, its bones preserved in shale or limestone in some Paleozoic creek bed for untold millions of years, would be more alive than the cold tuba in my hands. I recall that the frog who pretends to be my tuba was hibernating in my closet that is not a closet all weekend, and, in a final desperate attempt to avert disaster, I try to rouse him with a brief story.

"Once upon a time there was a handsome bullfrog who lived at the bottom of a pond," I tell him. "One day a beautiful princess came to the pond, and when he kissed her she morphed into a lovely frog babe. He thought he had found happiness and his one true love, but, whether princess or frog babe, she turned out to have a personality like a disease. This did not, however, mean that the bullfrog would never be happy. There are millions of other frog babes out there, in thousands upon thousands of other ponds. In fact," I tell my tuba, "the experience of having been disappointed once can actually be seen as a positive step, since important lessons have been learned, and the bullfrog will be much wiser the next time around."

The frog who pretends to be my tuba is not at all impressed by my story. He does not rouse himself from his torpor, whatever that means, but he does answer my story with a story of his own. "Once upon a time there was a boy who had a life that was not a life," he tells me. "He lived in a house that was not a house with a father who was not his father. His friends were not true friends, and basically he had nothing at all going for him. On the number line of boys, he was a zero, neither positive nor negative, neither whole nor fractional.

"Then one day a princess agreed to go to a basketball game with him. Fool that he was, he had a fleeting moment of glee. He thought he could become a musician, a scholar, a romantic figure. But something cannot be made out of nothing. Dust rose in the air, caught the rays of the sun for a brief moment and sparkled, and then returned to the earth as mere dust. The princess saw him for what he was and despised him. His father who was not his father trumped him at every turn. His friends who were not friends likened him to carrion. He was cruel to his teachers, who were sensitive, fragile people like himself, deserving kindness and respect. Ultimately, even his tuba could no longer stand to be played by him, so it committed brass instrument suicide in front of the entire band family—something that Professor Kachooski over there will no doubt confirm has never happened before in all the centuries of recorded music history."

I am not very cheered by my tuba's story to me, with its implied threat at the end. "Now listen up," I say to my tuba, shaking it slightly, "nobody's talking about committing suicide here. You and I are old comrades-in-arms. We've gotten through tough moments before. We marched, arm in arm, through 'The Gambol of the Caribou.' Suck it up, old friend. The tuba solo is only twenty bars long. We will make it through together. And here it comes!"

My tuba solo has arrived. In front of the band room, Mr. Steenwilly's head rotates completely around his neck several times, until it clicks to a stop facing in my direction. His eyes dart backward in his head, across the forest of curly black hairs on his scalp, down the Panama and Suez canals behind his ears, to meet again in back of his head for a quick check of old Professor Kachooski.

On his folding chair, the eminent musicologist is leaning forward, his right hand touching his golden right ear, as if to open that world-renowned receptacle a little wider so that my tuba solo can spill into it.

Mr. Steenwilly's eyes pop back into their sockets

like two excited weasels into their holes, and they focus on me. Up goes the Steenwilly right arm. Down comes his baton, signaling the moment of my entrance. "Come on," he is announcing, "this is your moment, O my chosen one. Blast forth on your tuba the notes that will confirm my place in the pantheon of modern composers, and win me the undying respect of my dear old professor and mentor."

The frog who is my tuba has other ideas. He sucks in a long, seemingly endless breath of pond air. His amphibious lungs swell, and swell further, until one more particle of oxygen will push even his capacity beyond the bursting point.

"Please," I plead, "do not do this to yourself, and to me."

"Goodbye, cruel world," I hear my tuba faintly gurgle . . . and then I believe the frog takes one final, fatal gulp of pond air. BAAAAA-BLAAAAMMMM! The air is rent by a shattering burst of sound so angry and forlorn and powerful that our basement band room quivers and nearly implodes, pushed to the very edge of what walls and ceilings in the physical universe can sustain. It is a sound that has never been heard in a band room before, since the dawn of time.

It does not actually fall within the range of sounds that a tuba can make. It is actually the concussive blast of a giant frog intentionally blowing itself to bits.

Mr. Steenwilly's mustache is blown clear off his face. It flaps helplessly around the room and comes to rest on a roof beam. His baton snaps in half, and his loafers disengage from his feet and sprint for cover toward the instrument-case closet.

Several feet behind him, close enough to ground zero to feel the direct effects of the explosion, Professor Kachooski is knocked out of his folding chair. He flies backward till he smashes into the front wall of the band room, and slides to the floor. The folding chair lands heavily on top of him, still standing upright, like a gravestone appropriately marking the final resting place of one of the great musicologists of the modern era.

I sit there, unmoving, unbreathing.

Several brave members of my band family play on without me for a few bars. Notes swirl around me like horseflies on a battlefield littered with blood and body parts.

"Play on," Mr. Steenwilly insists bravely, waving his

broken baton, trying to rally his troops. "The show must go on. It is the one unalterable, essential rule of show business. Here I stand, mustacheless, dishonored, yet willing to conduct you still! Play on, John."

I cannot, Mr. Steenwilly. It is all over.

One by one the instruments fall silent. A trombone is the last sad voice to falter and fail.

"John?" Mr. Steenwilly asks, stepping down from his conductor's podium. "Are you all right?"

There is now silence in the band room. I believe I see Violent Hayes watching me from one row in front, with very worried eyes.

Tears are beginning to stream down my face. I feel quite dizzy. "The frog is dead," I hear myself say in a very strange voice. I cannot look at Mr. Steenwilly, but I also cannot look away from him.

The members of my band family do not know what to make of my meltdown. I hear their whispered comments clearly, although they all seem far away.

"Why is he crying?"

"He said something about a frog being dead."

"No, a fog. He said there's a fog in his head."

"Must be a thick one."

There is some laughter. I hear it but I do not care.

I believe I am trembling. I drop my tuba and it clatters to the floor.

Mr. Steenwilly raises the broken half of his baton and brings it down with a slam on the metal platform that holds his sheet music. "*Silence*," he commands, and the laughter stops. "Band practice is over. You are dismissed for the day. Go! All of you." And then, more softly, "John, come, let's talk in my office."

But before anyone can move, an interloper of high status and stern demeanor suddenly invades our band room, entering purposefully through the door, striding resolutely up onto the band platform, and grabbing me around my shirt collar. It is Mr. Kessler, the assistant principal and chief disciplinarian of our anti-school, who, to my knowledge, has never displayed sufficient interest in music to honor us with his presence at one of our rehearsals before. But here he is now—a stocky man with a protruding jaw and thick white hair that he cuts so short it looks like a layer of permafrost which his scalp can never quite melt.

He yanks me up by the collar. "I hope you're proud of yourself," he grunts. "I hope you're very proud." And he begins dragging me toward the door.

"No, wait," Mr. Steenwilly cries out, bravely trying to blunt the anger of this officer from the high command. "You don't understand. We have a situation here—"

"Out of the way, Steenwilly," Mr. Kessler snaps.

"But this boy doesn't need to be punished," Mr. Steenwilly protests. "He may, in fact, need our help—"

"Back off. I'm handling this," Mr. Kessler barks at him. "And in case I need to remind you, I'm the assistant principal of this school, while you are just a junior faculty member, without tenure, who sometimes involves himself in situations he should stay out of. Don't push this any further. *Back off.*"

Mr. Steenwilly backs off. It is not that he is a coward. He is outranked and outgunned.

Mr. Kessler has me in one of those strangulation-by-the-back-of-your-shirt-collar holds they teach assistant principals at the Special Forces training grounds. He continues dragging me toward the door. A small shape suddenly looms up in front of him and interposes itself directly in his path. Someone in our band room is not afraid of Mr. Kessler! Someone yet dares to resist!

"Stop!" a bold voice orders our assistant principal. "This is a talented young musician who needs assistance, you barbarian!"

Mr. Kessler squints at this apparition who dares to order him around, and even to insult him, in his own domain. He sees in his path a small, old, bald man in a black suit. "Who the hell are you?"

"I am Kachooski!"

"Gesundheit," Mr. Kessler says. "And get out of my way."

"No, I am not a sneeze," Kachooski says, drawing himself up with great dignity. "And this talented young tuba player needs compassion. Trust me, I am a musicologist. I am, in fact, none other than Gustav Slavodan Kachooski!"

"Gesundheit," Mr. Kessler says again. "You might want to have that throat looked at," and then he shoulders Kachooski out of the way and drags me out the band room door.

I get one final glimpse into the band room before the door swings shut. Mr. Steenwilly stands there helplessly, his head bowed in defeat. As I watch, his hand opens, and the remaining half of his conducting baton drops out of his palm onto the band room floor.

21

the high command

As Mr. Kessler half leads and half drags me down the long main hallway, he gives me a little speech from his perspective as an educator who has seen many classes of students come and go at our anti-school. "I despise your entire generation," he begins. "I wish I could lift you off the ground and shake you by your puny shoulders like a pillow till the stuffing comes out the seams. I cannot, because in these dark days I would no doubt be sued for child abuse. But I wish I could do it. You need such a shaking, young man, and I'm just the assistant principal to give it to you!

"Back in the fifties, when I went to high school, we had respect. We believed in God and we knew he was watching us. We had a real enemy in Communist Russia, whose missiles were pointed right at the welcome mats in front of our neatly kept houses. And even if we danced to Elvis and disobeyed curfews now and then, we knew our parents were really right all along, so we listened and obeyed."

We are nearing the principal's office on the first floor. The bell to change classes has rung and teachers and students are crowding into the hallway, but they divide to either side at the sight of us, to give Mr. Kessler a clear path. They gawk at me as he drags me along by the collar, as one stares at an animal being led to the slaughter.

"Then the sixties came along with all their energy and madness," Mr. Kessler goes on. "I didn't like those hippies and yippies, but I respected them. At least they believed in something. I had a lot less respect for the disco heads of the seventies with their flared pants and vests, not to mention the shallow, materialistic yuppie wanna-bes of the eighties, but I could stomach them.

"But you and your whole generation I absolutely despise. Maybe it's because I am an old man now, nearing retirement age, but it seems clear to me that there has been a definite downward spiral within my lifetime, of morals and values and all the things I hold dear. And you and yours represent the bottom of that spiral. You are as low as I care to watch the youth of America sink. You stand for nothing. You respect nobody. The music you dance to is devoid of beauty, its lyrics empty of humor or cleverness. Your teen icons are pathetic. You have no love of parents, country, or God. You are the very worst kids that our great nation can produce, and I despise you one and all, you especially."

Of course, Mr. Kessler does not actually deliver this speech out loud. But I believe he is thinking it as his heels click off the polished floor of our anti-school. All that he actually says to me as we near the principal's office is "I hope you're proud of yourself."

He yanks open the door that leads to the main administrative offices of our anti-school and ushers me in. The principal's secretary, Mrs. Friendly, is filing her nails with what looks like a marlinspike. She puts the large file down at the sight of me. "So that's him?" she asks.

"That's him," Mr. Kessler agrees. "And not a word of apology or regret. He's actually proud of what he did."

"Well, I think it's disgusting," she says. "Just revolting. Stomach-turning. The principal is ready to see him." She gives me one final look. "And I'm glad I'm not in his shoes." And then she goes back to filing her nails.

Mr. Kessler drags me over to the slightly ornate door that leads to the principal's office. He knocks twice.

"Yes?" comes a voice from inside.

Mr. Kessler opens the door. "Dr. Whitefield? I have the boy here."

"Let him come in, and leave us."

Mr. Kessler pushes me into the principal's office and pulls the door closed behind me. I find myself standing in a large office, bathed in afternoon sunlight, its walls lined with bookshelves on which ponderous tomes about the philosophy and methodology of education strut back and forth like an extended family of pompous and ungainly penguins. The office is dominated by an oak desk of such size and polished to such a high sheen that I believe a regulation hockey game could be played atop it.

Sitting behind that desk is a man I have up till now only seen at a distance, when he has deigned to walk down our hallways, or to address us as an entire school body. But today I am facing him one-on-one.

Dr. Whitefield at first glance appears to be a rather unremarkable man, except for bushy eyebrows that sprout out above his eyes as if they have been expertly nurtured and manured and watered three times a day, season after season, till they have reached an unheard-of length and thickness, and he plans to enter them in a state fair.

The great shaggy eyebrows give him a peculiar look that is at once thoughtfully optimistic and deeply pensive, as if he, too, has been brooding about the direction of America's youth but, unlike Mr. Kessler, his angry assistant, Dr. Whitefield is trying desperately to think of creative ways to rescue us from the abyss.

"Be seated," he says. I sit down on a wooden chair, facing him. "I don't believe we've met before. What's your name?"

My vocal cords have gotten tangled up. "John," I somehow manage to croak out.

"So, John," he says, "you are the one." And he lets out a long, tortured sigh. "I don't mind telling you that this is the part of my job that I like the least. You know, young John, this may come as a surprise to you, but I went into education because I actually like children. Treat them well and they will treat you well, I always say. Never mind all these books, that's my educational philosophy in a nutshell. And then something like this happens. Oh, I know what I should do. I know what I have to do. But still, it is painful for me, and I hope you appreciate that. I am in pain right now."

I do not have much sympathy to offer Dr. Whitefield because I have just experienced a total meltdown, and there are still tears wet on my cheeks, and I believe I am still trembling. I also cannot speak, because my vocal cords are tied in knots. So I just nod.

"Nod your head at me, will you?" Dr. Whitefield demands, panic audible in his voice for a split second. "Well, you are an impertinent one! Do you think you can intimidate me with a little head movement? Do you see this button here on my desk? I have only to press it and Mr. Kessler and Mrs. Friendly will be in this room in five seconds to restrain you. And if they can't handle you, they will summon Mr. Waterman, the wrestling coach. So if I were you, young fellow, I would dispense with the arrogance and insubordination and just sit there and listen. You might learn something."

I sit very still and wait for Dr. Whitefield to speak. He is, after all, the only person at our entire anti-school with a Ph.D., and no doubt he has some important truths to share with me. We sit in silence for a long time. As he studies me, his forehead wrinkles toward the center, so that his eyebrows appear in momentary danger of tangling with one another, in which case I believe a landscape gardener would have to be summoned with hedge clippers to shear them apart. But gradually his face unfurrows and he opens his learned mouth. "I am in pain," he tells me again. "I hope you appreciate that. I feel personally wounded and put upon."

He waits for a response. I dare not nod my head. So I just sit very still and look back at him.

"Ice me, will you?" he asks angrily, slamming a palm down on the great oak desk. "All right, then, I've dealt with surly, incommunicative students before. This is a bad business, young John. Let's have an end of it. But you should know something. I grew up with Kitty Bradford. Bradford was the maiden name of your algebra teacher, Mrs. Gabriel. We all called her Kitty in those days—I can't remember exactly why."

A tiny blush of color appears in Dr. Whitefield's cheeks for a moment. When he speaks again, his voice sounds slightly softer in tone. "She was a lovely, gentle girl," he remembers. "We both went through this school system from kindergarten through high school. I was a few years ahead of her, of course, but I certainly knew who she was. I daresay most of the young men of this town took notice of Kitty Bradford."

He pauses, and licks his lips. Dr. Whitefield, were you sweet on Mrs. Moonface? Was she your Glory Hallelujah? Let me assure you, I meant her no harm. You and I are on the same side here, Dr. Whitefield. Even though I have had a meltdown and am nearly incapable of rational thought, you must believe that I would give my right arm if I could undo what has been done. Even though you have a Ph.D., you may not fully grasp that private thoughts are occasionally blurted out as spoken words without the necessary editing process. Harmful words occasionally force their way out of innocent mouths like floodwaters through dikes and dams, spoiling the best efforts of good people to contain them.

"Kitty Bradford was as smart and sweet and lovely

a girl as I have ever had the pleasure of meeting," Dr. Whitefield informs me. His fingers drum on the desk for a moment, as if counting back through the years. "Lovely and brilliant. She was a math prodigy, who won a partial scholarship to a famous college and probably could have gone on to make a significant contribution in her field. We stayed in touch, by occasional letter, during her college years." His fingers stop drumming on the desk and the office is suddenly very silent.

"I was a bit surprised when, upon graduating, she forsook more advanced mathematical training and chose to come back to this town and teach algebra, and to marry one of her high school classmates who was a noted athlete in his day, but perhaps not her equal in the intellectual sphere. At the time, and even more strongly when I later returned to this school system myself, in a high administrative capacity, I felt it was an unfortunate choice." He pauses, and I see him swallow and clear his throat. "But I suppose she loved him."

Again the fingers drum on the desk, I believe to mark the loss of years that could have been spent more happily. "Time passes," Dr. Whitefield muses sadly. "Day follows night. The best hopes of men and women are dashed. It's not for me to tell you, of all people, Mrs. Gabriel's trials and tribulations. But I will share with you that her marriage broke up several years ago, and that I believe it ended very painfully for her. And it's certainly no secret that she has a relatively serious medical condition with an attendant skin malady—which she has battled against bravely, but which has certainly affected both her health and her appearance."

Dr. Whitefield suddenly frowns at me, and jabs a finger in my direction as if ordering his eyebrows to go out and get me. His massive eyebrows obediently uncoil from atop his eye sockets, slither across the polished oak desk, wrap themselves around me like two anacondas from the Amazon basin, and hold me there so that I can barely breathe.

"*Mrs. Moonface*, wasn't it?" Dr. Whitefield demands. "Who can compete with teenagers for cruelty? Well, your outburst today in math class appears to have been the final straw. I was summoned to the ladies' faculty bathroom, where Mrs. Gabriel—Moonface to you—was having a breakdown. I fear she will not be teaching at our school for a while. I have relieved her of her duties so that she may recover."

He stands, and paces in front of the window. "And I am relieving you of your duties also. You are now suspended from our school. I would, if given half a chance, recommend expulsion to the Board of Education, but since no physical violence was involved, I believe they would not support it. So I shall have to settle for a week's suspension, to be followed by daily after-school detention and certain other penalties that I shall arrange as I have time to consider the matter."

He stops pacing and turns to face me. I believe our little session is almost at an end. "I must say," he adds, "that one of the most puzzling aspects of this particular case is that you seem to come from good people. I just got off the phone with your father, who impressed me. He is on his way here to pick you up. He was not at all pleased with what I had to tell him. He assured me that he will deal with you with a firm hand. And that's about all I have to say to you, John. Now do me a favor and get the hell out of my office."

22

floating

It is a strange thing to be suspended from school for a week. It really does feel like I have been upended and uprooted and that my feet are no longer on solid ground. I get up every morning, programmed by years of training to go to school, only to realize that school will not have me. The hours pass by slowly, with no school bells to kick them forward. I go for long walks through my town that is not a town, and through other nearby towns, and of course see no other kids my age. They are all in their classrooms, at their desks, rooted to their lives. I alone am suspended, hanging upside down like a bat left behind in an out-of-the-way corner of a dark cave, blind and isolated.

Every morning I wake up early and fix breakfast for the man who is not my father. And every evening I microwave dinner for him, and then clean up afterward. If he does not like what I prepare, or if my serving or cleaning skills are not up to par, he lets me know with a good hard WHOP.

You do not know me, so you cannot possibly know how I loathe this man. I hate his comings and goings, the way his boots thud on the floor when he enters or leaves our house that is not a house—I hate every mean or sly or angry word out of his mouth, and I even hate his silences.

The man who is not my father has followed up on his promise to Dr. Whitefield to deal with me with a firm hand. I am not certain whether the hand in question is his left hand, which he holds me with, or his right hand, which he WHOPS me with. A new form of punishment was introduced on Tuesday, which also required a firm hand. When he brought me home from school after my meltdown, he took me down into the basement, and he whipped me with his belt. His belt is broad and made of leather, and while it stung and reddened long bands of skin on my sides, arms, and legs, it did not cut or draw blood, so I believe the lashing left no permanent scars.

If you have never been whipped, let me assure you that it is more painful and far more humiliating than an occasional angry blow from a hand or kick from a boot. It is actually something that should probably only be done to vicious animals, and even then only as a last resort. You hear the person who is whipping you breathing deeply, because it is hard work to lash someone. You sense their arm drawing back and up. Then you can actually hear the belt whistling down at you, till it makes a loud WHAP sound as it stings your back or side. You do not think of resisting or running away, because that will only intensify the beating. All you can do is try to protect yourself, and wait for it to end. I took the blows crouching over, nearly kneeling, my hands in front of my face.

"If you're trying to screw up on purpose, to make trouble for me with your mother, I'm way ahead of you." WHAP. "You will never, ever, ever, screw up in school again, you little turd." WHAP. "You'll go back next week and be a perfect little scholar, and not a word of this to your mother. Or you'll regret it the rest of your miserable life." WHAP. "Do you hear me?"

"Yes sir."

WHAP. WHAP.

Since then, not an hour goes by, whether I am lying in bed reading, or watching TV, or walking through the streets of our town, when I don't suddenly remember that belt descending on me in our basement. I recall how my eyes, which I thought my school meltdown had drained of tears, squeezed out new ones as I held up my arms to protect my face. I remember how my vocal cords, which I thought were too tangled to produce loud sounds, produced loud, fearful whimpers. Most of all I remember the voice of the man who is not my father, and how much I hate him, and how completely powerless I was to stop him.

I am ashamed to admit that at least twice in the days since that beating I have had the clear thought that perhaps the frog who pretended to be my tuba was right after all. Perhaps an end to pain is better than pain.

On the outskirts of my town there is a five-story water tower. I climbed it on Wednesday afternoon and stood at the top, all alone. The wind blew and I put my arms out like a sail, and the sun shone and I thought, "Why not? Why not now?" I imagined with some pleasure sailing out high over our town. Perhaps I would land on the roof of my house that is not a house, and crash in through the bedroom shared by my mother and the man who is not my father, hopefully bringing the whole house down with me. Or perhaps I might sail in through the window of my anti-school, streaking like a comet into the office of Dr. Whitefield to come to rest in a crater right in the middle of his oak desk.

There are some detergents and cleansing products in the cabinet below our sink that, according to their labels, are highly poisonous. I am ashamed to admit I also considered mixing up the old witches' brew and taking a long, final gulp. That would get Mom home from Maysville on the first bus available. That would show Mr. Kessler and Dr. Whitefield that I am sorry for what happened to Mrs. Moonface. That would show all of them!

But I did not jump and I did not drink. Both of those are not honorable ways out—they are surrenders without terms. I hold this truth to be self-evident: An army has to keep resisting, even if the tide of the war has turned against it. Even if it is winter in Valley Forge. Even if it is dangerous, and painful, and so very, very lonely. One must go on fighting—it is the only honorable thing to do.

No one has called from school. No one has stopped

by—no friends, or friends who are not friends, or even enemies. As I say, no one has stopped, but twice I believe I have seen Mr. Steenwilly pass slowly by my house that is not a house in his old blue Chevrolet. I do not know why he keeps driving past. Perhaps my house is on his way home, and he always cruises by for a little sightseeing, but I have just never noticed it before. Or perhaps he has my house under some kind of personal surveillance.

My mother called on Wednesday night and again on Thursday. She knows nothing about my meltdown in school, or subsequent suspension. She is still out in Maysville, five hundred miles away. "Aunt Rose is getting worse" was the ominous news on Tuesday night. And on Thursday, "The doctors say she may not survive the night."

At four o'clock on this cold and bleak Friday afternoon, she calls a third time, with sad news. Poor old Aunt Rose has died. "She didn't suffer too much at the end," my mother tells me. "I'm glad I was here for her, to hold her hand. I was the only one. Poor Rose. Such a sweet woman, such a lonely life. I just have to wrap up some loose ends. We're going to have the funeral tomorrow, and there are some final legal matters to attend to, and then I'll be home."

The man who is not my father takes the telephone and exchanges a few final words with my mother in a sympathetic tone. If she could just see his face as he hangs up and mutters, half to me and half to himself, "Jackpot! Who would have thought the old gal had five thousand tucked away! I bet I'll find a way to enjoy it more than old Rose ever would have. I just hope your mom buries her cheap." And with those kind and respectful words, off he drives in his truck.

The man who is not my father has been away every day since my mom went to Maysville. I believe he is making use of my mother's absence to participate in an increased number of short hauls. He is, as they say, making hay while the sun shines. This is fine with me. The more he is away the better.

I seriously consider going to the police with my suspicions. It is possible, however, that the man who is not my father will temporarily give up all illicit activities, whatever that means, now that his wife-to-be is about to come into an inheritance. If I tipped off the police, and they placed him under surveillance and found nothing sinister—which seems more than likely, since he is a very clever man—I would become the villain. No doubt even my own mother would turn against me for telling tales to the police about the man she apparently loves and intends to marry.

This is the awful position the man who is not my father has placed me in: I know exactly who he is and what he is, but I have not a shred of evidence and no sure way to convince anyone else. For all I know, he is now off in his truck on a nature drive or an ice-fishing expedition. The only thing I know for sure is that he will be home sometime between eight and ten o'clock tonight, demanding his dinner as if he is some lord to whom I owe allegiance.

Four-thirty passes. I lie in bed trying not to think. Shadows change on my wall. Trees become clouds. Poor old Aunt Rose. But perhaps she is better off. Perhaps an end to pain is better than pain.

Five o'clock comes and goes. And then, at about five-fifteen, I hear a loud BZZZZ. Someone is at my door. I choose not to answer it. It cannot be good news. "Go away. I am in a state of suspension." BZZZ. Whoever it is is very determined. But I am more determined. "Go away. You are wasting finger energy pushing that buzzer." BZZZZZ. Whoever it is leans on the buzzer for ten long seconds. And then I hear a girl's voice calling me. "John, are you in there?"

It is a voice that I recognize, although I am surprised to hear it. So I get up off my bed and descend the stairs to the door.

Violent Hayes is standing there. "Hi," she says.

"Hi," I say back.

"I brought you some chocolate chip cookies," she says, holding out a package. I notice that the package has been opened, and two or three of the cookies appear to have mysteriously vanished. Still, it was a nice gesture.

"Thank you, but I am not hungry," I say.

"Well, you may get hungry," she points out. "Anyway, I brought them for you, so you may as well take them."

I take the package. "Thanks." Violent Hayes, what are you doing here? You have never come to my house before. I did not know you even knew where I lived. And, if I am not mistaken, you have even dressed up a bit. Are those earrings in your ears? Are you wearing a little makeup? What is going on? Don't you know that I am in a state of suspension?

"Aren't you going to invite me in?"

Violent Hayes, the man who is not my father may return home at any moment. For that reason, I do not do much entertaining at my house that is not a house. In fact, it has been more than a year since I have had a friend over. I believe the last person to come over to my house was Billy Beezer, long before we went to war. "Umm—let's take a walk," I suggest.

"Great," she says. "I like walks."

Violent Hayes and I walk for a long while in silence. She is a big girl and she takes big steps. It is a cold, bleak Friday, and the sun is setting, and I can feel winter coming on. We walk side by side down my block that is not a block, and I like it that she does not say anything. We turn right, and soon we are climbing Overlook Lane. There are more trees and fewer houses up here. My town that is not a town spreads out beneath us in a patchwork quilt of houses that are not houses and streets that are not streets.

"I've been worried about you," Violent Hayes finally says.

"I'm okay."

"Are you sure?"

"Sure I'm sure." There is a bit of anger in my voice,

and she wisely drops the subject of how I am.

"We really miss you in band. Mr. Steenwilly is going crazy without you being there to practice your tuba solo."

"I don't play the tuba anymore," I tell her. "I gave it up."

"Are you kidding? I love the way you play the tuba. It's so soulful. You're the best."

"My tuba is dead," I tell her.

Violent Hayes looks at me like she has just discovered that I am from Pluto. Didn't you know that before, Violent Hayes? Girls are supposed to be intuitive about such things. Did you have to see my green skin and the antennae in my head? "John, are you sure you're okay?" she asks.

"That's the second time you've asked me that stupid question," I snap at her angrily.

"Sorry," she says. "I just don't understand how a tuba can die."

"I need to go home," I tell her.

"Right now?"

"Yes. Now. Sorry."

We walk down the hill. Soon we are on my block,

nearing my house that is not a house. Violent Hayes stops walking. I continue on for two or three steps, but I cannot just leave her there, since she brought me a package of chocolate chip cookies, so I stop also, and turn back to look at her. "Sorry," I say, "but I have to go in now. Thanks for coming by."

"John?" Why are you looking at me that way, Violent Hayes? Your brown eyes have gotten as big as two butternut squashes. "Do you know what tomorrow is?"

"Saturday?" I guess.

"And what happens on Saturday?" she asks.

I shrug. I have no idea at all.

Violent Hayes, why do you look so nervous all of a sudden? I have never seen you nervous before. It does not suit you. A girl who can successfully wrestle with a monitor lizard on a regular basis should not be nervous, but I believe you are trembling. "The Holiday Dance," she says.

Oh, yes. The Holiday Dance. I recall that I once entertained a rather vivid fantasy of squiring Glory Hallelujah to that fabled event. I believe we will, in fact, not be going this year. It does occur to me that

Glory Hallelujah has sworn an oath never to speak to me again for the rest of her life, so if I did ask her to the Holiday Dance she could not actually say no to me, which she will never get a chance not to say, because I will not ask her. "Oh, yeah," I mutter. "That stupid dance. Right."

"Are you going?"

"No," I say. "I hate dances. And I don't know why they call it the Holiday Dance, since the holidays are still far away. But most things are not what they seem. You see my house over there? It is actually not a house at all. But I still better go into it."

Violent Hayes is looking at me as if she has just discovered that I am not from Pluto but actually from another galaxy entirely. She is definitely trembling. Violent Hayes, it is a cold afternoon, and winter is coming on, but why oh why are you shivering and shaking so that even your big brown eyes seem to be trembling? "You could go with me," she says.

"No," I say. "I . . . I don't know how to dance."

"I don't care," she says. "I don't know how either."

I am looking back into those two brown eyes, as big and soft as two butternut squashes. "It's semiformal, right?" I say. "I don't have anything good to wear." I do not add that I had some good clothes, but I left them in a basement and they were burned by a bulldozer.

"You're about my brother's size. You could borrow some of his clothes."

"I'm broke. I couldn't afford two tickets right now."

"I'm asking you," Violent Hayes says. "It's my treat."

"I cannot go. I'm suspended from school."

"It's not in school. It's in the town hall this year."

Oh, Violent Hayes, those eyes of yours are killing me. Turn them off. Pull the blinds down. Don't you know that the man who is not my father has given strict orders that I must be home in the evenings to prepare his dinner and clean up afterward? Don't you know that it is now against the law for me to have any fun? Do you have any idea of the consequences if I disobey? "I'm sorry," I say. "I can't go. I really can't."

She looks at me. There are tears welling in the corners of those big brown eyes. "But, John, you have to."

"Why?"

"Because I don't have anyone else to go with," Violent Hayes admits, and I can see how hard it is for her to say this. "And I really want to go. I've never been to a dance before. Never." She blinks and takes a few quick breaths. "And, John, I really want to go with you."

23

No-View Alley

The Saturday of the Holiday Dance dawns gray and cold, and by noon it is snowing. The flakes drift in from the north, at first thin and dry as dust specks, and then increasingly thicker and wetter.

"Sky dandruff," the man who is not my father grunts. He is apparently not a snow enthusiast. "Roads'll be lousy. Last thing I need." He drives off in his truck at four o'clock, which is a good thing. I thought I might have to sneak away, but he has saved me the trouble.

Left alone, I begin to wonder what I will wear to the evening's festivities. Violent Hayes kindly offered to lend me some of her brother's clothes, but I feel strange about showing up as her date and asking for handouts. I ransack my closet that is not a closet, looking for hidden clothes that might have fallen into cracks and corners over the years and been forgotten about.

Now, if my closet were a real closet, I'm sure there would be some stray clothes lying around that would be perfect for a Holiday Dance. Aren't people always saying, "Look what I found at the bottom of my closet. A silk dinner jacket! I forgot it was even there. And it still looks so nice!"

But my closet is really a kitchen or a bathroom masquerading as a closet, and there is nothing at the bottom of it but an old sock with a hole in the toe, a boot that I believe Sprocket, my dog, has mistaken for a bone and gnawed on, and a tennis racket with broken strings. So I unfortunately do not have the wherewithal to even attempt to make myself presentable.

The shoes that I was forced to abandon near Glory Hallelujah's couch have no good substitutes—I squeeze into a pair that I have had since I was twelve years old. They feel at least a size too small for me, and their heels have been worn down to tiny misshapen stumps, so that I have the strange sensation that I am heading downhill on one shoe and uphill on the other. I believe that even Fred Astaire, in his prime, could not dance in these shoes.

My gray corduroy pants were ripped in the knees

during my escape through the pet door and my crawl down the passageway, and then further frayed during my long night of loading cartons. I consider trying to sew them or patch them, but in the end I just put them on. So what if my right kneecap is visible? It is a fairly attractive kneecap, after all. I have no good shirt, no good sweater, and no good jacket to wear, so I put on this, and I button up that, and when I look in the mirror I find that I resemble a scarecrow who has been standing out in a cornfield too long, so that even the crows pity his wardrobe options.

No matter. Violent Hayes wanted me and she is going to get me. I have decided that, suspension or no suspension, threats from the man who is not my father notwithstanding, I am going to go to this dance. I am feeling a strange kind of courage. It has been building all day, and now, in my own odd way, I am feeling quite brave. Of course, deep down I recognize this courage for what it is—pure foolishness. Essence of stupidity. But so what? When your life that is not a life keeps getting worse and worse, eventually you reach a point where you have very little left to lose. Wearing Essence of Stupidity like a cologne, I head out the door.

Who is this scarecrow walking down Main Street in shabby shoes and raggedy pants? Who is this young vagabond who shuffles slowly along Grandview Lane, checking his watch every time he passes under a streetlight? I do not recognize him. Is he a clown from the circus? Is he a beggar checking the curb for pennies and nickels that have fallen out of people's pockets? He cannot be me. Even I would never try to pick up a girl for the Holiday Dance looking this pathetic and decrepit.

And there Violent Hayes's house is, on a flat stretch of Grandview Lane, hunching so close between the houses on either side of it that the three of them appear to be leaning on each other for mutual support against the winter wind. I must confess that I do not know why they have named Violent Hayes's block Grandview Lane, since there is not a grand view or even a petite view, and it is more of an alley than a lane. It should be called No-View Alley.

The clown trips on the nearly nonexistent heels of his shoes that are not shoes and falls in the gutter where he probably belongs. Ah, so it is me, after all! I get up, knocking snow and clinging particles of mud from my hands and knees. My fall into the muddy gutter has not improved my appearance. I hurry the rest of the way down No-View Alley and turn up the walk to Violent Hayes's house.

I draw back my fist to knock on Violent Hayes's door, but she opens it before my knuckles connect with the wood. I cannot stop my fist from moving forward, and I believe I bop my date for the evening right in the nose. No matter. Violent Hayes has what I believe boxers call an iron chin. She takes my best shot, and actually smiles. "Wow. Hello to you, too," she says. And then, "Don't you look great."

I check over my shoulder to see if there is some other guy standing on her stoop. Violent Hayes, I do not know who you are seeing standing on your doorstep, but if he looks great, he is clearly not me. You, on the other hand, have gone to some trouble to doll yourself up. I do not believe I have ever seen you in a dress before, Violent Hayes. Green may well be your color. And whatever you have done to your hair is rather fetching.

"Come in. John, this is my dad. Dad, this is John."

I did not think it was possible, but Violent Hayes's father is even more massive than the Bulldozer. On the Richter scale of fathers, he is a major earthquake.

He must weigh nearly three hundred pounds, and very little of it appears to be fat. He has a shining, slightly reddish face, as if he has imbibed one too many drinks at some local bar, and his arms are so long they seem to almost graze his knees as he walks forward to meet me, giving him the friendly appearance of a slightly inebriated mountain gorilla.

Mr. Hayes, Your Gorillaship, let me say right off the bat that I do not have a very good record in establishing friendships with the fathers of my dates, but I hope to change this immediately. I would also like you to know, Your Apehood, that my feelings toward your daughter are more than chaste. To me, she is like the sister I never had, and did not want, but I do not mean that in a negative way. While I admit that I have started off badly, by showing up dressed like a scarecrow who has been banished from his cornfield for slovenliness, I intend to be the perfect chaperon. I will bring Violent Hayes back to you on time, well danced, and I promise there will be no hanky-panky. There will not even be any panky.

"So you're the fellow Violet never shuts up about?" Mr. Hayes asks me. But he is wearing a grin.

"Daddy," Violent Hayes says. But she is wearing a smile.

He pumps my hand. I have never shaken hands with a mountain gorilla before. It turns out they are remarkably gentle beasts, with great shaggy paws. Of course, I have never seen one when it is provoked, but I also have no intention of ever doing anything that may in any way irritate this gargantuan specimen of fatherhood.

"Come on upstairs, then, John, and let's see if we can fix you up with a jacket," Mr. Hayes says. "The old wife couldn't be here to meet you, but she left out some of Donny's clothes that should fit you okay."

"Donny's my brother," Violent Hayes tells me as we climb the stairs. "He doesn't live here anymore, but he keeps some clothes here for when he visits."

Soon we are in a small upstairs bedroom where several jackets have been laid out on a bed. Ah, yes, this is indeed a fine selection of men's clothing, Mr. Hayes. This navy blue blazer with the brass buttons looks quite sharp on me, if I do say so myself, except for one small problem. Your son, Donny, while almost my size in terms of height and girth, has apparently inherited the arms of a mountain gorilla. "Those sleeves are going to be a problem," Violent Hayes says.

"He can just roll them up," Mr. Hayes suggests helpfully.

"Daddy, that would look stupid."

"It doesn't matter how you look, or how people look at you—what's important is how you look at yourself," Mr. Hayes declares, and I notice that his own shirt is not completely tucked in.

I would like to copy down this pearl of wisdom for future generations, but unfortunately I did not bring a pen or paper.

"Daddy, don't you have a game to watch?" Violent Hayes reminds him.

"Oh, yeah. Halftime is probably over." Once again, I am offered a mountain gorilla paw. "Nice to meet you, John. Have fun, you two. Dance up a storm, and try to stay off each other's feet." And off he goes, lumbering down the stairs.

"I guess I could try a quick fix," Violent Hayes muses. She disappears into her own room, and returns a moment later with a sewing kit. She pins here and stitches there, and in a matter of moments the navy blue blazer fits me as if it had been designed for me. Violent Hayes, you have some unexpected talents. "Let's go," she says. "The dance started half an hour ago. They've probably already crowned the Winter Queen, and things are probably heating up!"

24

the Holiday Dance

Who are this young couple who hurry along through the cold winter evening? The wind is whooshing, the moon appears to be wearing a muffler of gray clouds, and the snow is so heavy and wet it seems almost flocculent, whatever that means. But the two young people who hurry along toward the town hall do not seem to notice the bitter weather. They are not holding hands, nor are they fixing each other with lingering glances, but they appear happy enough. I believe I even detect occasional bursts of laughter from their direction.

They reach the town hall. The young woman opens her purse and purchases two tickets, while the young man checks out his reflection in a conveniently placed wall mirror. His shoes and his pants are shabby, but his snappy blue blazer more than makes up for them. His image in the mirror is suddenly joined by the reflection of a large girl in a bright green dress, who puts her hand in his own. "Well, John," Violent Hayes says, "are we a pretty spiffy couple, or what?"

"Indeed," I say. I do not mention that "spiffy" is an adjective I usually associate with very clean frying pans.

"Here's your door prize," Violent Hayes says, and hands me a candy cane. No, on second glance, I see that it is actually a commemorative pen cleverly disguised as a candy cane. Imprinted on the pen, in black letters that stand out against the red and white stripes, are the date and the location of this Holiday Dance. I stuff this valuable keepsake in some pocket or other, so that I will have proof to show my grandchildren that I attended this important social event.

Violent Hayes and I, our hands still linked, follow the sounds of loud music down a long corridor. We are approaching a set of double doors that lead to the party room when the doors burst open and a pair of enormous eyebrows walk out, stop suddenly, and arch angrily in my direction. No, these eyebrows are not entirely disembodied. Hidden somewhere beneath them, I spot the torso and legs of Dr. Whitefield, the principal of our anti-school, whose duties apparently include policing the Holiday Dance.

Now, Dr. Whitefield, before you throw me out of this hall, let me remind you that the theme of this party is the holidays. There is, if I am not mistaken, a Santa hat perched precariously on your head. Surely Santa would not take an action so contrary to the holiday spirit as booting me out of this dance into the bitter cold. Surely you will welcome me with good cheer, and not make a scene in front of my date, and in front of this short woman who has just followed you out the double doors, and who I assume is the woman you married when you gave up waiting for Mrs. Moonface.

"What the hell are you doing here?" Dr. Whitefield demands.

"I am here for the Holiday Dance, sir," I say.

"You can't. You're suspended. Get out."

Violent Hayes interposes herself between Dr. Whitefield and me. "He's suspended from school," she points out. "This isn't school." Violent Hayes, are you risking your neck for me with the principal of our anti-school? Do you think I can't handle this myself?

"Who are you?" Dr. Whitefield asks her.

"I'm his date."

"Well, then I pity you," Dr. Whitefield says.

I consider saying that I pity Mrs. Whitefield, but I decide to keep that to myself for the time being.

Our pleasant little encounter is suddenly given new energy when a man with two cameras bouncing around his neck runs up, out of breath. "Dr. Whitefield? Are you ready for your photograph?"

The two great eyebrows swivel in his direction. "What photograph?"

"The one for the front page of tomorrow's *Star Ledger*," the man gasps. "With you and your wife, and the mayor and his wife, standing in front of the town Christmas tree."

"Oh, that photograph," Dr. Whitefield says. "The mayor, huh?" I notice Dr. Whitefield's fingers adjusting his tie. "Well, I hate to keep the mayor waiting, but as you can see, I'm attending to very important administrative matters here."

At this point, the short woman who I believe is Mrs. Whitefield asks, "Did you say the front page, young man?"

"Yes, ma'am. It will run in color on the front page. The mayor and his wife are already in front of the tree."

No doubt Dr. Whitefield would prefer to discharge

his disciplinary duties first and pose for a picture afterward, but the short woman who I believe is his wife grabs him by the arm, hoists him over her head, and carries him off at the speed of light in the direction of the Christmas tree.

Violent Hayes smiles at me and in we go through the big double doors.

I do not know if you have ever been to a Holiday Dance in a town hall, so allow me to paint the scene for you. We find ourselves in a large and high-ceilinged meeting room, paneled in dark wood, that has been decorated with streamers and tinsel. Tables with platters of cookies and giant punch bowls have been set up in the corners and along the walls.

Bing Crosby is crooning "White Christmas," while a few brave couples waltz in front of windows beyond which the thickly falling snow is visible. No, scratch that. It is not Bing Crosby, it is a rock song; and couples are not waltzing, they are dancing. No, scratch that. It is not a rock song—it is hip-hop and pounding rap and grinding, ear-splitting industrial rock, and couples are not just dancing, they are boogying and slam-dancing and moshing in what looks more like combat than dancing.

Violent Hayes, I was happy to escort you to the Holiday Dance, but let me remind you that I myself am not a dancer. No one has ever taught me how to dance, and that may be a good thing because I believe I have no ability whatsoever. The sad truth is that I cannot even stand still in time to music. Furthermore, I am wearing shoes that are not shoes, they are torture devices designed to create blisters and make me lean to one side or the other like an indecisive Tower of Pisa. To attempt to dance in such shoes would be nearly suicidal, and I have recently sworn off suicide.

Violent Hayes, are you leading me out to the very center of the dance floor? Did you not hear anything I was saying? Violent Hayes, are we waltzing? Is this your soft body pressed up against my own? Are we boogying? Are we moshing? Has the room tilted, or am I now standing on the wall? Is this really music, or a grenade assault? Is this moshing, gyrating mass of adolescent energy a high school dance or the first battle of World War III?

We take a breather. I get Violent Hayes a glass of punch, and have one myself.

"Wow," Violent Hayes says, "you're a great dancer.

Where did you get those moves?"

Violent Hayes, I learned those moves from watching nature shows on television. Those are, in fact, the exact contortions a wildebeest manifests when it is being devoured alive by a pride of hungry lions. "Oh, I don't know," I say. "I was just trying to follow the music." And then I ask her, "Do you know Mindy Fairchild and Toby Walsh?"

"I know who they are, sure, but I don't think either one has ever said a word to me since third grade. Why?"

"Because I believe they are about to join us," I tell her.

And, indeed, our school's star athlete and resident beauty are walking in our direction. She is wearing some sort of absurd tinsel and mistletoe tiara, having apparently been chosen Queen of the Holiday Dance earlier in the evening. Toby, amiable as ever, thumps me on the back. "Hey, John," he says, "saw you out on the floor. Didn't know you were such a dance machine!"

Toby, I am not a dance machine. I am not even a dance windmill or a dance waterwheel. But tonight I am wearing Essence of Stupidity as a cologne, and it has made me fearless. "Well, you know how it is," I say.

"That's such a lovely green dress," Mindy tells Violent Hayes. "You look really pretty in it."

"Thanks" is all that Violent Hayes can manage in reply. But I believe these kind words from the most popular girl in our anti-school make Violent Hayes grow a foot taller, and her face suddenly beams like a sunburst.

Mindy turns to me. "Say, John, you haven't seen Gloria around?"

"No," I say, holding on to Violent Hayes's hand. "And I haven't been looking for her, either."

"Well, she was supposed to be here. She's bringing this new date. She wanted me to meet him. Chuck something."

"Wagon?" Toby suggests helpfully. "Steak?"

"No." Mindy giggles, and bats her athletic escort on the shoulder. "His name is Chuck Woodblock, or Woodbridge, or Bridgewood. He's some big football player at State College."

"And he's chasing high school girls? He must be really hard up," Toby observes. "Come on, Dance Queen, I like this song," he says, pulling Mindy out onto the floor. As they pass me he mutters, "Go easy on that punch, Johnny boy. I think somebody spiked it."

Ah, that explains why the dance hall is spinning. That explains why the next hour or so of the dance passes by in a slightly hallucinogenic whirl. That explains why my eyes seem to flash like two disco balls, and why the room seems to get smaller and then bigger and then smaller again. Are we having fun, Violent Hayes? I believe we are. Is that Billy Beezer dancing with Karen Dirigible? Did he just come over and shake my hand and say no hard feelings? Is that Andy Pearce fast asleep under the punch bowl table?

At exactly eleven o'clock I am out in the middle of the dance floor when I suddenly dance right smack into a wall. No, it is not one of the walls holding up the ceiling of the town hall. The wall that I dance into is movable—it has, in fact, moved to get in my way. The wall that I dance into is, in fact, the massive chest of a young man who is, I believe, following the directions of his date. The young woman in question is wearing an expensive and rather slinky blue ball gown. The gown has been cleverly designed to just cover all the curves and straightaways of Glory Hallelujah's nubile body without very many stitches to spare.

"Well, look what the cat dragged in," Glory Hallelujah says, her gaze lingering on my torn pants and shabby shoes.

"Excuse me," I say, "but I am busy dancing with my date."

"I think before you do any more dancing, you owe me an apology," Glory Hallelujah's husky companion informs me. "You just bumped into me, peewee."

"No," I correct him. "Actually, you bumped into me."

He grabs me by the shirt collar. "Is that right? Well, I hear you used to go out with Gloria. And I hear you didn't treat her very well. And when Chuck Broadbridge hears something like that, it makes him real mad."

But before Chuck Broadbridge can say anything else I hear a loud KEE-WAK sound, unlike anything I have ever heard before, especially during a Holiday Dance. It sounds like the earsplitting crack of a bamboo trunk snapping in half before hurricane winds. Chuck Broadbridge lets out a scream and begins hopping on one leg. Upon reflection, I believe the sound had nothing to do with splintering bamboo but was actually generated by the impact of Violent Hayes's high-heeled right foot connecting with Chuck Broadbridge's left shin. "She kicked me!" he gasps. "I can't believe it. She kicked me. She could have ended my football career!"

"And I'll kick you again if you don't leave my date alone," Violent Hayes tells him, targeting his right shin for a possible second strike.

Glory Hallelujah steps forward. "Oh, big John, the soccer star," she says. "So you have to hide behind a girl, huh?"

"I don't have to hide behind anyone," I say, making sure to keep Violent Hayes between myself and Chuck Broadbridge at all times.

"If you say another word, I'll kick you, too," Violent Hayes warns Gloria.

"You wouldn't dare, you, you . . . water buffalo. Is that a green dress or a golf course?" Gloria asks her with a mean little laugh.

"You can't make me feel bad, you feather-headed ostrich-faced piece of expensive garbage," Violent Hayes tells her. "You're the one who should feel bad. You had the best boy in this whole school, and you let him go, and you didn't deserve him for one minute. Now get out of here or I'm really going to kick you."

Violent Hayes draws back her leg menacingly and

Glory Hallelujah and Chuck Broadbridge beat a hasty retreat. They take up a fallback position twenty feet away, and begin pointing at us and conversing angrily, as if trying to work out who is to blame for their rout on the battlefield.

At that moment I spot two enormous eyebrows cruising around me in tighter and tighter circles, like a shark scenting blood. I believe that Dr. Whitefield may have witnessed the shin-kicking episode, and he may be planning to top off his evening with a late double ejection from the Holiday Dance.

"Violet," I say, "it has been a lovely evening, but perhaps we should head home now."

She glances at her watch. "Wow," she says, "it's after eleven! You're right, we'd better go. I think I've had about as much fun as I can possibly have in one night."

25

gotcha

Who are this young couple that walk together up No-View Alley, hand in hand, completely unmindful of the whooshing wind and the flocculent snow? They appear to be old friends, or perhaps new lovers—interestingly enough, in the Lashasa Palulu language, the two terms are rather similar.

Newly fallen snow lies several inches deep on the rooftops and sidewalks and lawns, a glistening and pristine white carpet that muffles their footsteps and turns their conversation to whispers, so that it is hard to tell what they are talking about. I am quite sure they are speaking utter nonsense to each other, but they appear to be having a very good time.

They reach a house that looks like it needs to lean against the houses on either side of it for support against the wind. "Why don't you come in?" Violent Hayes offers. "I'm sure my parents have gone to bed by now. We could have some hot cider and watch TV in the basement." Violent Hayes, your eyes are gleaming in the moonlight.

Ah, the young fellow is tempted. But he has learned a thing or two in his brief life that is not a life. "I would love to," he says, "but it's late, and as you said yourself, it would be hard for the evening to have been more fun. So let's say goodbye now."

"Okay," she says. "Okay." She hesitates. The moon discreetly hides its face behind some clouds. "John, will you kiss me good night?"

"I'm not sure it's a good idea," I try to warn her. "I am a notorious nose biter. A lip nipper, and perhaps even a tongue chewer."

"It's a good idea," she says, closing her eyes and moving her head forward.

Violent Hayes, is this a kiss? It feels so soft and warm. I did not know that kisses came in this flavor. Ah, so this is why people like kissing. Now I see, now I see!

"Good night, Violet. Here's your brother's jacket back."

"Good night, John."

Who is this young fellow in the shabby shoes and

the ragged gray corduroy pants who is floating home from the Holiday Dance? How is it possible that he can walk home through the newly fallen snow and leave no footprints? It must be a hovercraft pretending to be a fourteen-year-old boy, and this happy whistling sound must be some open valve releasing steam from the hovercraft. Oddly enough, the steam from the hovercraft seems to be whistling the melody to the tuba solo in "The Love Song of the Bullfrog."

The boy reaches his block that is not a block, trips on a curb, and falls face first into the newly fallen snow. Ah, so it is me after all. I get up looking like Frosty the Snowman and laugh at my own clumsiness, a jolly happy soul indeed. In fact, I am more than jolly—I believe I am filled with glee—which is a very dangerous way to be. In fact, if you live in a war zone, there is no more dangerous combination in the world than being slightly drunk on spiked punch, filled with glee, and wearing Essence of Stupidity as a cologne.

I approach my house that is not a house. I am so filled with glee that I do not conduct the necessary reconnaissance. I just open the front door and start to walk in, when a hand reaches out and grabs my right arm in a painful grip. "Gotcha!" a voice says, and I smell the whiskey reek of the man who is not my father.

No, in fact, this does not happen. Just as I did not go down into the basement with Violent Hayes and incur the wrath of her mountain gorilla of a father, I do not try to enter my house that is not a house without conducting the necessary reconnaissance. You see, as I mentioned a moment ago, I have learned a few things in my life that is not a life. First, I note that the man who is not my father's truck is not around. This is a very good sign. Then I circle the house, peeking in the windows. The rooms are all dark, and the TV is not on. This is another good sign.

I walk halfway around the house, and see no signs of life. My house that is not a house is quiet, dark, and, to all appearances, empty. I reach my backyard, pass the apple tree that is actually a gray-leaf tree, and stomp through the ankle-deep snow to my back porch. I quietly climb the steps, open the door, and slip inside. But as I reach to turn on the light, a hand shoots out of the darkness and grabs my right arm in a painful grip. "Gotcha!" a voice says, and I smell the whiskey reek of the man who is not my father.

I attempt to pull away, but there is no escape from his grip. "Hello, John. Do you happen to know what time it is?" he asks, with mocking politeness. I get the feeling that he has had quite a bit to drink.

"After eleven," I say, looking around for someone to shout to for help, or for an escape route, or even for a weapon. But we are all alone at the back of my dark house that is not a house.

"Any idea what I had for dinner?" he asks.

If I do shout, I believe the falling snow will muffle my cry for help. And I know I will not get a second chance. "No," I say, "I don't know what you had for dinner."

"Nothing," the man who is not my father says with a laugh. And then his grip on my wrist grows tighter, and yet tighter. "Nothing at all."

"There's food in the fridge. You could have cooked something for yourself—" I break off then, as my wrist is twisted almost completely around.

"You give me lip, you're gonna make it worse for yourself. Where have you been all night?"

"At a dance," I gasp.

"Yeah, right, as if someone would want to dance with you. I'll teach you to mind me. I'll make you dance." And he begins to drag me along the hallway, toward the door to the basement.

I have a sudden very vivid flashback from our last visit to the basement—I feel his thick leather belt lashing my back and shoulders as I try to ward off blows to my face. My body recoils from the memory, and I yank away from him. Somehow, I loosen his grip on my wrist . . . and then his hand is gone completely. I am free.

"Flee!" the little man who sits at the control switchboard of my brain types into his keyboard at high speed. "Legs, churn. Arms, pump. This is a do-or-die moment. Get going!"

But my freedom is an illusion. I did not break the man who is not my father's hold. He is merely shifting his grip on my wrist to a much more painful one. His right hand darts forward, and before I can flee, I am lifted clear off the ground by my hair. I cry out in pain, and my feet kick thin air.

I do not know if you have ever been suspended by your hair with every ounce of your weight contributing to your agony. It is excruciating. I am being scalped by the force of gravity.

The man who is not my father takes a step toward

the basement. And then another step. We are right near the door to the basement stairs. "Dancing, huh? I'll teach you to mind me," he says again. Even in my agony, the stench of his whiskey breath is sickening. He is quite drunk.

I hear a sudden growl, and then I am released from his grip so suddenly that I fall heavily to the floor. I see that my loyal dog, Sprocket, has bitten the man who is not my father's leg, and is still in the act of chewing on it. The man who is not my father tries to kick Sprocket away. When this fails, he reaches down, picks Sprocket up by a hind leg, and hurls him into a wall. Sprocket lands in a heap and makes a terrible whimpering sound—I fear he will not be able to come to my defense again.

But he has gained me a few valuable seconds. This time I do flee. I dodge around my distracted tormentor and make a dash for the front door. "Stop!" the man who is not my father calls. "Stop now or by God you'll regret it."

I hear him coming after me. I believe that he is limping. Sprocket has done some damage.

Suddenly I find myself playing the doomed victim in one of those B horror movies where the teenager is chased around his own house by a limping, murderous monster. Surely, you would think, I could outrun a man whose leg has just been gnawed on by a dog. But I appear to be running through our house in slow motion. The man who is not my father is coming after me, cursing wildly, and gaining with each step.

I reach the front door. It is locked. My fingers fumble with latches and bolts. There, finally, the door flies open!

The man who is not my father grabs me from behind. He spins me around. WHOP. The blow with his open hand catches me on top of my head and makes my vision blur and my ears ring.

But I have a surprise for him. I have come up with a weapon. Unfortunately, it is not a knife or a gun. It is, in fact, the keepsake pen disguised as a candy cane that I was given as a door prize at the Holiday Dance. Without even thinking what I am doing, I raise it and slash at his face. I aim for an eye, but I believe that in the darkness I miss. I can feel it sink into the soft flesh of his cheek.

The man who is not my father's hands go up to his face. Even in the darkness of our front hall I can see that I have drawn blood. It is said that bullies become frightened or squeamish when they are made to feel pain themselves, or when their own blood is drawn. Don't believe it. The man who is not my father has an opposite reaction—he becomes so enraged that he loses all control. He utters a loud roar and strikes out at me with a closed fist.

BA-BAM. I have never been punched by a grown man's closed fist before. The impact lifts me off my feet. The good news is that he launches me in the direction I wanted to go—I fly out the door and land on our front porch. The bad news is that I taste my own broken teeth and bits of bloody lip. I do not have time to conduct a more extensive inventory of damage because the man who is not my father is coming out after me.

There is no escape—he is faster than I am. I cannot possibly defeat him in a fight—he is far stronger than I am. Nor can I outfox him—he is craftier and meaner than I am, and I believe he has decades of experience in all manner of fights and brawls.

Unfortunately, I have no other options.

Among the Lashasa Palulu—that tribe that is not a tribe—there is a saying that roughly parallels the

English expression "I will fight you to the last drop of my blood." It is used only in situations of complete hopelessness, when a cruel enemy will not negotiate, and when even a divine intervention such as an eclipse is not a possibility.

Now, some might say that continuing to struggle against an overpowering enemy is an act of foolishness that can only increase and prolong pain. Some might suggest begging for mercy, or curling up in a fetal position, shutting your eyes, and accepting your fate. But the Lashasa Palulu believe that if you are truly cornered by a merciless enemy, and all hope of flight or being saved vanishes, you might as well go out bravely and with an act of noble defiance.

Let me add here that I am still wearing Essence of Stupidity as a cologne, which is not a bad thing if one needs to commit an act of noble defiance. Also, I am still, perhaps, slightly drunk from Holiday Dance punch. And lastly, a very nice girl was heard to remark earlier this evening that I am the best boy in my school, and crazy as that claim was, her words and her tone have stayed with me.

Instead of running away, I step forward to meet the charge of the man who is not my father, trying for another slash at his face. He did not expect me to come forward. KA-POW, our bodies collide awkwardly, and the force of his greater momentum carries us both down the stone steps of my front porch—BAM, BAM, BAM—into the snow.

The fall separates us . . . and we get to our feet at about the same time. He roars deep in his throat—a low, enraged animal sound of pure menace. I scream back at him at the top of my lungs. I do not scream words—I scream hate. As he comes for me, I do not run away from him, but rather I run to meet him, trying to knock him off his feet. I windmill my arms crazily at him, and I feel my right fist connect with what I hope is his face.

But the man who is not my father also connects with a punch, and his blow knocks me flat on my back. All the air vanishes from my lungs. I try to roll over . . . to stand back up . . . but it is impossible to move without any air in your lungs. And suddenly he is pinning me down with his weight, and choking me with both his hands around my neck.

I cannot get him off me. I kick at his back, and claw at him feebly, but it is no use. He is a man and I am a fourteen-year-old boy. I see his fist draw back and then come forward. It looks as big and heavy as a wrecking ball. BA-BAM! The punch breaks my nose. I can actually hear the bones crunch.

He is killing me. The good news is that it does not hurt as much as you might think to be killed by someone you hate, if you go down fighting. I am still kicking at him and fighting back, but so much of my blood is now in my face that I cannot really see anything. Then I hear an unexpected voice: "Get off him, you villain. OFF, I SAY!"

Someone is trying to pull the man who is not my father off me. The tiny corner of my brain that is still able to function identifies it as Mr. Steenwilly's voice. "GET OFF HIM!" Mr. Steenwilly shouts again. "I called the police! They're on their way! GET OFF HIM!"

I believe that the man who is not my father attacks Mr. Steenwilly. There is much shouting, and the sounds of blows being struck, but I am no longer sure exactly what is transpiring around me.

I hear the long, twisting wail of a police car's siren heading up the block toward us. I sink deeper and deeper into that swirl of sound, and the dark, cold night closes over me.

who I am

N₀, I am not dead, I am just at the bottom of a pond. It is a deep pond, and I seem to be all alone down here.

At the bottom of the pond of consciousness, at the deepest part, it is just barely possible to see lights and to hear sounds. The lights are not glaring, and the sounds are not annoying when you are down this deep. All is peaceful.

Leave me down here for a while, please. I am enjoying it on the bottom of the pond. I have never seen the underside of a lily pad before. Please do not summon me to the surface just yet.

"John? John?"

I float back up to the surface very slowly. There are tiny golden air bubbles all the way up. I break the surface of the pond of consciousness and see bright lights and faces. Ah, hello, Doctor. Ah, hello, Mr. Policeman.

The pain hits me like a hammer.

I cannot sit up or even move my head because I have been tied down to the bed, like Gulliver, by dozens of different restraints. Ropes and wires and plaster casts and tubes seem to go in and out and around every part of my anatomy.

I believe my nose is now on the side of my head, and there is a bandage over one of my eyes, and I cannot tell if I have any teeth left in my mouth because my tongue is either asleep or in a plaster cast.

"John? Can you hear me? Can we talk to you? Squeeze my hand if the answer is yes."

I float in and out of consciousness. I try to listen to the police and to answer their questions, but I do not know if I help them. They appear to have done an impressive amount of criminological investigation without my assistance. They found a load of stolen TV sets in the back of the man who is not my father's truck. They have also found his gun in his sock drawer. It turns out he has a police record. They ask me if it is true, as one of my teachers suspects, that he has been abusing me for a while.

I squeeze a hand and sink back, away from all the questions.

Goodbye, police. Goodbye, doctors. I float down for a nice long stay at the bottom of the pond.

"John? John?" I float back up, against my will. Hours have passed, perhaps days. The people in my room have changed. I see my mother bending over me. I have never seen such concern in her face as I see now.

Behind her, through a small window, I believe I see other familiar, concerned faces peering in at me from a waiting area. Perhaps I am imagining it, but I believe I see Violent Hayes out there, and Mr. Steenwilly, and even, if I am not mistaken, dear old Mrs. Moonface, holding some flowers.

"John? Oh my God! Are you in pain?"

I cannot speak, Mother. I cannot even nod. I will blink one eye. There. That is your answer. Yes, I am in pain.

"Baby, they say . . . the police say this has been going on . . . for a while. That's not true? It can't be true?"

A blink. Did you get that, Mother?

"Oh my God! John, why didn't you tell me?"

A friendly doctor comes up behind her. "Ma'am, I think that's enough for now."

My mother ignores the doctor. She is holding me tightly by the shoulders as she repeats her question. "Why didn't you tell me?" And her voice is getting louder. It is almost a wail. "Why oh why didn't you tell me?" And her face is inches from my own, and I think she is even starting to shake me, or maybe she is the one who is shaking. "*Why didn't you tell me?*" she demands, and there is both anger and pain in her voice.

A very strange thing happens. I believe I have no teeth left in my mouth, and I am not even sure I have a tongue, and my jaws have been wired shut, so that I cannot speak. And my arms are all tied up with restraints so that I cannot move a muscle. But suddenly, somehow, I grab her back, and I open my mouth, and in an awful croaking whisper, I answer her with a single word: "Him."

"Him what? What are you saying?"

Somehow I manage to whisper out five words, slowly, each one an effort. "You—would—have—chosen—him."

Now I believe that three doctors are trying to pry her off me, but with no luck at all. "No," my mother says, shaking her head, "*never. How can you even say that?*"

I cannot speak out loud anymore, so I answer her without speaking, looking right into her prematurely old, pained, loving, angry eyes. "You did choose him," I tell her. "You love him. You brought him into our house. You're going to marry him."

My mother is no longer shouting or shaking me, but she is still holding me very tightly. Even though I didn't speak out loud, she heard me and understood. "Don't you know?" she asks me back. "Don't you know who you are?" Tears are sliding down her cheeks and falling off onto my face. I never knew how hot someone else's tears feel. "You're part of me," she says, as if it is the deepest truth she knows. "You're all the family I have. The only person I can count on. You're flesh of my flesh and blood of my blood, my only baby, and nothing else comes close to that. Nothing."

And then she runs out of words, so she just clings to me, and not all the doctors in the world can pull her away. I look back up at her, and yes I am in pain, and yes I am groggy, but I have no desire to return to the bottom of the pond quite yet, because I am feeling something that goes beyond pain or glee.

You see, I could hear the truth of it in her voice, and I can see the truth of it in her eyes that are still dripping hot tears over me.

So it appears that I was wrong all along. From the very beginning—from my first four words in this angry little tale of woe—I was wrong.

Oh my long-suffering mother, with your lost youth and faded beauty, and all your frustrated hopes for love and family with the man who was my real father, and with the thousands of hours you have logged at the factory, which I know you hate, each hour more painful than the one before it, each day and each week a burden—I look up into your eyes and I see the truth there, and I admit that I was mistaken all along.

So you do know me, Mom.

So you do know who I am after all.

Epilogue,
whatever that means

There is a good crowd on hand for the Winter Concert. I have made a miraculous recovery, and have healed enough to be sitting in my old spot in the brass section, holding my tuba that is not a tuba, watching Mr. Steenwilly conduct his way through the opening bars of "The Love Song of the Bullfrog."

When my solo comes along, I am nervous that my chipped teeth and wired-together jaw will put a damper on my rendition, but I have underestimated the magical healing power of music. "Just play, and it will all take care of itself," Mr. Steenwilly advised me before we went onstage, and, indeed, that is exactly what happens once I start. With five hundred people listening, I nail the tuba solo. When I finish, with one last, lingering, throaty note, the audience does not wait for the piece to end. They erupt with applause and a chant of "John! John! John!"

Unfortunately, none of this actually takes place. I am indeed at the Winter Concert, and the band is about to play "The Love Song of the Bullfrog," but I am not seated onstage with the other members of the band family. It is impossible to play a tuba when your jaw is wired shut and there is a plaster cast covering much of your face. I still cannot eat solid food. I cannot whistle. I cannot hum. And I certainly cannot play "The Love Song of the Bullfrog" on my tuba that is now a tuba.

My tuba has become a tuba because it is now being played by one of the most eminent musicologists of the modern era. I will tell you how this came about.

Apparently, my severe beating at the hands of the man who was not my father was reported in several local newspapers. Old Professor Kachooski read about what happened to me, and the man with the golden ear also turns out to have a golden heart. He called up Mr. Steenwilly to find out what hospital I was in, and then he came to see me and asked if he could have the honor of filling in for me at the winter concert.

"There is a long and honorable tradition of one

musician sitting in for another in emergency circumstances so that the show may go on," he explained. "The tuba was one of my first instruments. And Arthur has worked so hard on that piece—we really must find a way to do it justice, and let his frog sing. If you don't mind."

I nodded my agreement. The show must go on. I have reminded myself of that basic truth many times during my rather painful convalescence. There have been several operations involving reconstructive surgery and dentistry that have left me with long hours of throbbing pain.

"But I have one condition," Kachooski added unexpectedly. "Since you practiced this piece so hard, and since I understand the solo was written for you, I would like to play it on your own tuba—as a sort of testimonial to you. If you don't mind."

I debated telling Kachooski that my tuba is dead—that he was present, and in fact blown off his chair, at its demise. But I decided to keep this information to myself. After all, he is a world-renowned musicologist with a golden ear, and I am a fourteen-year-old boy with a mashed face.

So now I am sitting on the fifth bleacher of our

anti-school gymnasium, with my mother on one side of me, and Violent Hayes's mountain gorilla of a father on the other. On the bleacher just in front of me sits good old Mrs. Moonface, tapping her toe to the beat as our band wraps up a march by John Philip Sousa. On this cold winter evening our band sounds remarkably good. It is a strange thing—I never practiced my tuba much, and I played in the band only because I was forced to do so by the high command of our anti-school, but I now find myself wishing very much that I was up onstage.

Arthur Flemingham Steenwilly skewers the end of the Sousa march with a few deft final swipes of his baton, and turns to face the audience in his new black coat with shiny buttons. The tips of his mustache, which have, I believe, been trimmed and waxed for this important occasion, bungee-jump down from his face to turn the page in the score in front of him and then spring back into place. He smiles out at us—it is clear that he has brought much light to our anti-school in his thankless crusade.

"We would like to play one final piece for you," he says. "I ask your indulgence—it was not written by a famous composer but by a young man with a lot to

learn. It is called 'The Love Song of the Bullfrog.' "
He begins to turn back to the band, and then stops
and clears his throat. "This piece features a tuba solo.
It was written for a promising musician in our band
who cannot perform it tonight, but he's here in this
hall, and we'd like to dedicate it to him. John, would
you please stand up."

I did not expect this. I do not particularly want to
stand up. My face—never a work of art, even in its
best days—is still black and blue from the beating
that the man who was not my father administered. I
believe several of my most prominent facial features
have been permanently rearranged. A large cast hides
the most egregious damage, and I have wished that it
was even larger—that it covered my entire face
except, perhaps, for a breathing hole and two eye
slits. The best thing to do with a face like the one I
am wearing on this winter evening is to keep it well
hidden.

But everyone is looking at me.

"That's you, Johnny boy," the mountain gorilla
exclaims.

"Go ahead," my mom says. "Stand up."

Suddenly I find myself on my feet. I duck my head

once or twice in some kind of an awkward bow, and sit back down again as quickly as I can. The crowd is so pleased that the boy with the mashed face has sat down and the concert can now continue that they break into applause.

"They're clapping for you," my mother says.

No, Mother, they are not clapping for me. They are clapping for themselves to appease their own guilt at having done nothing to prevent my brutal treatment. That is why Dr. Whitefield is standing and clapping so hard that his massive eyebrows shake like tropical flora raked by typhoon winds. That is why his sadistic second-in-command, Mr. Kessler, applauds with the same hands he used to drag me down the hallway. Glory Hallelujah is also standing, but I do not believe she is clapping at all—I believe she is using this opportunity to stand and show off her new slinky outfit, which may indeed not be clothing at all but, rather, body paint on naked skin.

My mother unexpectedly leans over and gives me a kiss. She does not actually make contact with me— she kisses a corner of my face cast. I twist away and say "Mom," because public displays of affection from mothers are strictly prohibited in our anti-school gymnasium, but I suppose it is not an entirely bad thing that she is fond of her son.

Mr. Steenwilly turns back to the band and raises his baton. Down comes his right arm, and the piece starts. On my right side, I can feel the mountain gorilla tense up, but he need not be worried. Violent Hayes nails the opening saxophone interlude. She is looking particularly fetching tonight in a long blue dress, with a red ribbon in her hair, and I suppose the monitor lizard that pretends to be her saxophone is as charmed as I am.

Andy Pearce follows up with the drum segue. I hear a few minor traffic violations. There is a long screeching of tires. One jarring fender bender makes Mr. Steenwilly wince, as if a ferret has just crawled out of the kettledrum and bitten his ankle. But Andy has done far worse in his time.

Meanwhile, the tuba solo is swimming toward Professor Kachooski like a giant stingray with a few thousand volts to spare. But even from where I sit, I can see that eminent musicologists have no fear of solos, stingrays, or even tubas that are really dead frogs. Kachooski is a pro. At precisely the correct millisecond, he begins the solo.

Oddly, no music comes out of his tuba that is really my tuba. There is no love song at all. Instead, I hear the disembodied voice of a dead frog—a ghostly, amphibious voice that floats out over the large hall, speaking to me and me alone. "Once upon a time there was a boy who was lucky enough to survive a war, but not wise enough to count his blessings," the voice says. "He had a mashed face and he wanted to hide it from the light. People clapped for him and he remembered old wrongs. Foolish lad, he had survived a war and expected the world to be a beautiful and blissful place.

"But," the disembodied frog continues, "a war zone remains bleak, even after the last gun has been silenced. The boy's real father will not suddenly appear—he is probably in jail or dead. Algebra will still be algebra, with its many hairy legs and poisonous pincers. His friends will still on occasion liken him to carrion, and no doubt for good reason. Antischool will still be anti-school. Members of the secret sorority of pretty fourteen-year-old girls will still turn up their noses at him, if given half a chance."

Kachooski is nearing the end of the tuba solo. His old face has turned red with the effort of sustained exhalation, whatever that means, but despite his best efforts he is still not producing any music. The disembodied frog voice speaks faster, and in a slightly more encouraging tone. "The boy should not, however, be completely dismayed," the voice says. "There are, occasionally, a few bright moments that flash in the darkness. Lily ponds buzzing with fat flies on autumn evenings. Algebra teachers with pasty faces but good hearts. Brave pet dogs who try to protect their masters despite peril to life and limb, and who now keep them company during their convalescence. Mothers who try to cheer up their hospitalized kids by playing checkers with them, and repeating silly jokes they heard at the factory that day. Saxophone players with ribbons in their hair and brown eyes as big and soft as butternut squashes. And if the boy learns to recognize such moments, and savor them, infrequent and transitory though they may be, he may find they make the whole shebang worth while."

Kachooski plays a long, last, lingering throaty note and lowers my tuba. The crowd, still and silent as stone statues, listens as if a magical spell has been cast over them. There must be dust in the gymnasium, because I find that my eyes are wet. Mr.

Steenwilly accentuates the last notes of his masterpiece with a few final dramatic flourishes of his baton and then turns to the audience, and bows.

People stand and clap. I remain seated, self-conscious about again showing off my many bruises and ridiculous face cast. My old and tired mother, who is not known as a big music fan, jumps to her feet and claps as if her palms have caught fire and she is trying to beat out the flames. The mountain gorilla also stands and pounds his massive paws together, beaming proud glances at his daughter. Violent Hayes looks back at him from the stage, her face shining. Her gaze swings from the mountain gorilla to me, and for a moment we have a little silent communication, just the two of us. It may be a good thing that I am wearing a face cast, because I believe I am blushing beneath it.

Among the Lashasa Palulu, that tribe that is not a tribe, battle heroes who have been wounded in action are never given medals. They wear their scars as the proof of their bravery, and at village festivals they are seated in prominent positions and expected to lead the celebrations.

Mashed face and all, I stand up and clap with the

rest of them. As I blink away the puddles of moisture that my eyes are pumping out, no doubt to dispel the irritation of airborne dust, I am forced to admit that Mr. Steenwilly caught a true emotion and set it down in sharps and flats, and Kachooski nailed the tuba solo for him. And I understand that, forlorn and cautionary as it started out, and muddled and painful as it became in places, it was, in the end, a love song.